Julie's Secret

Julie's Secret

Cora Taylor

GREYSTONE BOOKS
Douglas & McIntyre
Vancouver/Toronto

Cover illustration by Richard Burkholder
Cover design by Robert Grey
Edited by Peter Carver

Greystone Books
A division of Douglas & McIntyre Ltd.
1615 Venables Street
Vancouver, British Columbia V5L 2H1

Printed and bound in Canada
96 95 94 93 6 5 4 3 2

The publisher acknowledges the support received for this
publication from the Canada Council.

The author wishes to thank Marilyn Wallace and
acknowledge assistance from the Calgary Public Library
Writer-in-Residence program co-sponsored by the Alberta
Foundation for the Literary Arts.

This book was published originally by Western Producer
Prairie Books, a publishing venture owned by Saskatchewan
Wheat Pool. First Greystone edition 1993.

Canadian Cataloguing in Publication Data

Taylor, Cora, 1936–

   Julie's secret

   Sequel to: Julie.

   ISBN 1-55054-124- 2

   I. Title.

PS8589.A883J83 1993   jC813'.54   C93-091600-X
PZ7.T39Jul 1993

For my granddaughters: *Terry Jean Ritshard*
August Christine Vida
Lisa Ann Taylor
Erin Beth Sullivan
Katie Grace Taylor

Chapter One

Christmas morning Julie opened Jimmy's present last. It was wrapped in wrinkled green tissue paper. The kind that came in the box of mandarin oranges.

The Morgan children had taken their mother's decree of a home-made, re-cycled Christmas with a good deal of grumbling at first. They understood the need for economy. Since Will Morgan's accident there had been what he called "a tight money policy."

"But Christmas . . ." as Jane pointed out when they were told there'd be no gift allowances, "Christmas is Christmas!"

"Seven children to buy presents for and gift allowances for seven *times* seven is just too much!" Alice Morgan said firmly.

Mary's suggestion that they draw names was voted down. It always was. The Morgan children agreed that it was more fun to get lots of little presents from each other. In the past they had been able to come up with some amazing gifts for only a couple of dollars.

Still, there had been grumbling and not much action in the Christmas department until one weekend when Charlie was home from university in Edmonton.

"You wrapped Mum and Dad's present in a paper bag and tied it with binder twine?" Mary was incredulous.

Charlie grinned. "Sure, and I'm going to wrap yours in a piece of the week-end comics and tie it with old typewriter ribbon!" After that, originality became the Morgan motto, not just for presents but for the wrapping too. Which explained why the living room floor this Christmas morning was littered with little traditional wrapping. Instead there was everything from newspaper to toilet paper (Jane's wrapping for her gift to Joe).

1

Julie was peeling tissue like the skins off an onion. The package had decreased from soccer ball to softball size when she realized Jimmy had moved over beside her.

"Careful," he said, "it's breakable."

"She'd never have guessed," giggled Jane, "what with the *Handle with Care* and *Fragile* stickers you put all over the outside!"

Julie realized that everyone was watching her. She carefully unwrapped the last few layers and saw the china dalmation.

"I fixed your dog," Jimmy said.

Julie stared at it. It was the dalmation she had taken to the tree the day of Will's accident. The special dalmation from her dog collection.

"I found it under your pet tree, when it fell. You can kinda see the glue marks and one leg was too smashed to fix but it was missing a leg before . . ." His voice trailed off. ". . . So I figured you wouldn't mind."

Julie stared at him. "You kept it all this time? Ever since September?" It was incredible. She'd thought it was shattered beyond repair and had not even gone to look for it. Had not wanted to go, really, after the tree had fallen. Could not go at first, remembering the storm and the fear.

Jimmy looked uncomfortable. "Well . . . I knew it was special. You never used to carry any of the other dogs around . . . and sometimes I'd see you holding it." He grinned. "It looked like you were petting it or something! So . . . well, anyway . . . I figured it was special."

Julie could feel tears gathering. Funny how when you had four brothers you might not really notice one. Everyone knew about Jimmy and his passion for horses. But she realized she was seeing a side of him now that he kept carefully hidden from others.

"It was special. And . . . and it's just about the best present I ever got!" She set the dog, still nestled in its tissue paper, carefully on the floor and threw her arms around Jimmy.

"I think," said Alice Morgan with a proud smile, "there have been some very thoughtful and special gifts this Christmas. If we were having a competition it would be pretty hard to pick a winner."

"Right! I know I'm really going to enjoy mine from Jane!" Joe jubilantly waved a snapshot of Jane with a dish-towel. On the mounting paper underneath was written, "I will take your turn at dishes for one month. (Signed) Jane Morgan."

"By the way, I'll choose January . . . February's too short!"

Mary held up a piece of soap carved in the shape of a nurse's cap. "I love Billy's soap carvings to everybody. You're getting pretty good too!"

"Some came out better than others. I tried to do a tractor for Dad but the wheels kept breaking off. . . ." Billy's voice trailed off. Too late he remembered how close a tractor wheel had come to taking Will Morgan's life.

Silence circled the room as each member of the family remembered that day. The overturned tractor with Will pinned under it, his narrow escape from death and long convalescence, and all of the struggle to keep the farm going. Suddenly the tight money Christmas seemed a small price to pay for the gratitude they felt at having him there.

Alice Morgan glanced at her husband, swallowed hard, and said brightly, "Never mind, Billy, the truck you carved was fine and the horse's head you carved for Jimmy is a masterpiece. You must have put a lot of time on it."

"He figured Jimmy hardly ever washes his hands so the soap would last a long, long time!" Joe chortled.

"I think my soap is perfect." Julie held up a leaf, the veins intricately carved.

"I couldn't find green soap dark enough to be a balm of Gilead. That's why I had to do springtime poplar. . . ." He examined the soap critically. ". . . Even then it's kinda the wrong shade."

"It's perfect." Julie smiled at him. This was the brother she knew best. The two youngest, they spent a lot of time together in spite of the fact that they were opposites in almost every way. When they were younger Julie had envied Billy because he was "normal." While she was struggling to cope with being different, she had clung to Billy for the security of his common-sense, unimaginative view of the world. He was her home base even when she knew he did not understand or even recognize the strange knowledge that she was attempting to sort through in her life. She carefully set the soap down and looked again at the mended china dog still swathed in its tissue wrapping. Glancing at Jimmy, she hoped he had not noticed that she hadn't picked it up yet.

The truth was, Julie was afraid to touch the dalmation. Afraid to know how it felt after all this time. The day of the accident seemed now to be like a dream—a memory, indistinct and unreal. She knew part of this was because she willed it so. She was afraid to relive the fear and tension. But it was more than that. She did not shrink just from reliving the events. It was the knowledge of what she had done and the fear of learning how she had done it that made her pull back. Somehow that day she had touched something, hooked into something so vast and frightening she could not even bear to think about it.

She hadn't had to at first. For a few glorious minutes after the storm took her tree down she had been filled with exultation but just as suddenly that was gone and she felt limp and wasted. Unable to think or care—or remember. It was as if her body and mind had been drained of all thought and strength. When Alice came home from the hospital after Will's operation Julie had collapsed in her mother's arms. After a week of watching Julie's listlessness and lack of energy, Alice had taken her to see the doctor on one of her trips to see Will, who was still in hospital in Red Deer.

Dr. Barnes shook his head when he saw her. "A body would swear that you'd had an operation just like your dad. Except he's coming around a good deal faster than you are, young lady!" He turned to Alice, "Nothing too serious. Rest and a tincture of time ought to do the trick. Must be the aftermath of shock at finding her dad under the tractor." He patted Julie's shoulder. "You haven't been running any marathons and not telling us!"

Julie tried to join in their laughter but her laugh had no life. The prescription had been to stay home from school for at least two weeks. That solved part of the problem.

With her mother shielding her the questions changed. "How

4

did you know Dad was under the tractor?" became: "Boy, it was sure lucky you got there when you did!" "Whatever possessed you to ride that crazy stallion?" became: "Good thing you decided to ride Diablo and he ran away with you!"

Only once did Alice Morgan herself ask a question: "Do you know how you do it, Julie?" Not specifying whether "it" was knowing things from past or future or the stranger, stronger things Julie had done that day.

Julie, lying propped up in bed, had simply looked at her mother with misery in her eyes and shaken her head, sobbing softly as if too exhausted or bewildered to do anything else. And Alice said no more, only held her, rocking and saying over and over, "It's all right . . . just rest," until Julie fell asleep.

Now between mother and daughter there was no more talk than there had been in the days when Julie was afraid to speak of the things that bothered her and Alice had feared the knowledge and power her daughter possessed. But in their silence there was reassurance and there was much unspoken—a look, a hug, the touch of hands when they were near.

Everyone said Julie perked up once Will was home from the hospital. With the help of the neighbours organized by Paddy Behan, and with Charlie missing a week of university, the harvest had been done. Only doctor's orders and Alice's constant watchfulness kept Will from getting involved with the work. Even then, once or twice he insisted that he could haul grain and would have if he could have figured out a way to climb into the truck before the pain stopped him. Having Charlie home was a mixed blessing. Both his parents worried about him falling behind in his courses.

"Boy's taking agriculture, so combining twelve hours a day while the weather holds ought to count for one course!" Paddy said. But Alice had been relieved when Charlie announced in November that he was caught up at last.

By the time Julie went back to school the other Morgan children had already borne the brunt of local curiosity about Will's accident. A more recent level crossing accident near

Lacombe that took the life of a former Hurry resident now claimed everyone's interest.

Julie wondered why no one noticed that she was different. Perhaps she hadn't changed that much on the outside. After all she had always been quiet, a loner. So no one noticed that she was withdrawn now. Only Julie knew that she was not the same as before.

Part of it was deliberate. Julie was guarded, vigilant, always watching her thoughts.

She felt like a water beetle skittering along on the surface of things. If I don't look hard, I won't see things other people don't. If I don't breathe too deeply, I won't smell things that are not there. If I don't think or concentrate I won't . . . but she was not even sure what she was avoiding. Only that she hoped never again to feel the way she had in the days after Will's accident.

So she quietly left the living room carrying the china dog still lying in its bed of tissue paper. She sat on her bed, staring at the dalmation in her lap.

Once, the ornament had been warm; special and somehow comforting. She remembered that once she had even thought it might have power like Aladdin's lamp. Jimmy must have been watching then, if he thought he'd seen her petting it. That was why she'd carried the dog out in the storm after the accident that day.

Chapter Two

"Julie!" Jane's excited voice came up the stairs. "Come on! We're going horse skiing. It's a perfect day!"

Julie looked out the window. It was true. The sun was bright, and the snow sparkled as if someone had sprinkled jewels over it. Puffy snow covered the roof of every shed and granary, making them look picture book perfect. Even the dog house, with Sport's head poking out, looked special.

"C'mon, Julie." Billy was at the door. "It'll be the first time in ages we all go. Charlie's going to use Diamond and Jimmy will take Pinto so there'll be two ropes. You can be behind me!" He rushed down the hall to his room.

Ever since Julie was little the Morgans had gone horse skiing on the east quarter whenever there was a fresh snow and time to do it. She didn't even know when Charlie had invented the sport. They'd always done it although they were the only family she knew of that did. All that was required was a horse, a long rope, and kids on skis. Charlie or Jimmy would be first in the line holding the long driving reins as well as the tow rope. The others just spaced themselves along the rope and hung on. There was a set order in which the Morgan children lined up. The ones who fell down the most were at the end of the line so they didn't trip everybody else. Julie had spent her entire life being last on the tow rope.

She was a much better skier now, because after all she'd be eleven in May. But she was still the youngest and still the most likely to fall.

She remembered times when she was little and she would inevitably come home from horse skiing, ignominiously sitting on her tied-together skis because the others got fed up stopping every time she fell down.

For years Julie associated skiing with the feel of snow pushing up inside her sleeves, a cold, wet-wrist feel from falling hand first in the snow. Still, no one ever got hurt. All you had to do was let go the rope in time.

She really didn't want to go today but she knew she'd never get away with backing out. And it was a rare treat, everybody going together. Besides you couldn't go just any time you felt like it. Conditions had to be exactly right. You couldn't, for example, go if the snow was packed and drifted. It made the field treacherous and uneven. And the snow had to be the right depth. Deep enough to cover the stubble and no bare spots. You needed a field that was flat. Steep hills made you get up too much speed and run into the horse. The east quarter was perfect but last year they hadn't been able to go there because it had been summer-fallowed and the lumps of dirt were just too big and too many to avoid.

She could hear the door slam and Jane's voice, "Get a move on, Julie!" before the door slammed again.

There was plenty of activity in the yard now. Diamond and Pinto were being harnessed, the rope attached to the surcingle. "I'd swear that horse enjoys tearing around the field with those kids trailing behind," Julie remembered Will saying. She was sure he was right. She used to listen to Diamond's chuckle-snort every time he had to stop for her when she fell and think he was laughing at her.

She watched as Joe grabbed a too exuberant Sport and led him back to the doghouse to be tied up. They'd learned the hard way that Sport's enthusiasm and horse skiing did not mix. At first they'd been amused as he cut between them, back and forth as they skied. But when Diamond broke into a gallop and they began to go faster the inevitable pile-up had occurred. Now, they always left the yard to the tune of Sport's mournful dog-left-behind howl.

Billy was standing at the bedroom door. "Hurry up, Julie!" He crossed to the shelf where she kept her dog collection and took something out of his pocket. "I noticed when Jimmy was

8

fixing it that your dog's now missing both his hind legs, so I fixed him a stand." He placed a block of wood, carved with a bit of hollow in the top, on the shelf and stood waiting for Julie to put the dalmation in place.

Julie took a deep breath. There was no more time to wonder whether the dog would feel warm or cold to her touch. Now she would know if the dog still had the power she had sensed before or if it too had changed.

She took the dog out of its tissue paper and carried it across the room to where Billy stood waiting.

The dalmation was warm.

Flesh and blood warm the way it had always been. She gently touched each of the other dogs, feeling their china or plaster coolness with her fingers. Even the carved wooden puppy was colder.

She realized that there was no sense of relief that the dog was the same and wondered if she had been hoping that it would have changed too. Still, there was no disappointment. Only the familiar feeling that something was not normal, something that she did not understand. It was a feeling she had known ever since she could remember.

She turned and followed Billy down the stairs.

Julie stood for a moment on the step outdoors adjusting to the glare of sun on snow. She shut her eyes and breathed the fresh winter air. It smells of sunshine, she thought. Clean and clear and more than that. It smells the way the snow looked from the window, glittering and brilliant.

Chapter Three

"Last one again!" Jane called from her place behind Joe. The two horses stood waiting, Pinto pawing impatiently, Diamond standing firm but looking around to see why Charlie was still holding him back. Joe and Jane were holding the rope behind Jimmy. Behind Charlie, Mary and Billy had spaced themselves leaving a spot at the end for Julie.

She ran over and got into her skis as Pinto set out, Jimmy holding him to a walk with difficulty. It was hard enough negotiating the ruts and icy patches in the yard, and nobody wanted to fall down in sight of the house. They all knew their parents would be watching. Any signs of irresponsibility would go hard. Although the Morgans owned two skidoos, Alice Morgan had firmly forbidden any suggestion of replacing the horses after one of Mary Behan's city nieces had cut her face on a barbed wire fence while on a toboggan towed by a skidoo.

So the Morgan skiers left the yard sedately. They usually cut across the pasture and up through the hay meadow to get to the east quarter. It meant opening and closing two sets of gates, and Will was wintering cattle in both fields this year so there would be bare spots and lumps of manure to dodge. Today Jimmy suggested they take the road a quarter of a mile and then turn east down the old road allowance. Christmas morning there would not be much traffic, and they promised Alice they would keep to the side. Normally there would not be enough snow even there but the county snowplough hadn't come by yet.

Once they were out of the yard and up the road a bit, Jimmy let Pinto into a trot. It was really easier that way. A walk meant going at a jerky pace, half skiing and half being towed. There

10

were hazards to skiing beside the road. Sticks, branches, or fallen fence posts hidden in the snow could trip a skier.

Everything went smoothly until Joe caught his ski on something, went down, and Jane, trying to avoid him, wiped out in the ditch. Diamond, following Jane, did not need Charlie's "whoa!" to bring him to a sudden stop. Julie hadn't been paying attention and before she could stop had gone up the slack in the rope and knocked Billy down. The first reaction each of them had was to look back to the house.

"Do you think Mum saw that?" Mary worried.

Charlie laughed. "Not unless she's up on the roof with the binoculars!" Everyone relaxed.

Jane lay on her back in the ditch. "Oh bilge!" she said. "Stupid snotgurgle!"

Joe was on his skis ready to go. Gazing at the sky, whistling nonchalantly as Jane climbed out of the ditch and flung her skis down. "Decided to take a little side trip did you?" he asked innocently.

"Never mind, broccoli brain," she said. " *You* had the first fall!"

"First fall! First fall!" Jimmy yelled. The others joined in. It was a ritual. They always cheered the first fall.

Julie had always thought they were just trying to cheer her up because it was usually her. This time she got to join in. She felt an unfamiliar bubble of happiness in her chest. Once the first fall was over you could relax a bit. She beamed at Charlie as they started to move again. It was a nice day.

"We should always come this way," Mary said as they turned down the old road allowance. Once there had been a dirt road here, but now there was just a single track passable only in dry weather. Nobody used it in winter. Poplars and choke-cherries now grew in from the fences on either side, making a narrow lane.

The horses were moving at a fast trot now, and Julie had to concentrate on keeping her skis straight. She could hear the others talking and laughing, Jane and Joe trading insults and threats, Mary asking Charlie what it was like living in Edmonton. She'd be off to take nursing after graduation.

It would be strange without the two eldest. Nobody'd realized how much Charlie contributed to the farm and family until he was gone. It had taken both Jimmy and Joe to take care of his work, made even heavier by Will's convalescence. Julie supposed Mary's work would fall on Jane and her. Their mother must be dreading that. Mary worked with quiet efficiency and never complained. Julie was famous for her inefficiency and Jane never did anything without complaining. They'd be a discouraging team.

Julie wished things didn't have to change.

"Almost to the turn," yelled Jimmy. "Watch it!"

"Slow down!" called Charlie, holding Diamond back to a walk. "We have to stop and open the gate."

Pinto and Jimmy disappeared around the bend. Julie knew there was another, sharper turn up the bank to the field gate. She could hear Joe's yell and Jane's "bilge again!" and a few other words from Jimmy that it was just as well his mother couldn't hear. And then they came around the bend themselves.

It looked like a battlefield. Bodies everywhere. Joe was tangled in his skis in the ditch, Jane lay sprawled face down in a snowbank, and Jimmy was lying, his skis tangled in the barbed wire gate that had been left lying across the gateway partially hidden by snow. Pinto had only run a few steps before the dragging reins brought him to a stop. Now he came back to nose his fallen master.

Jimmy was getting stiffly to his feet as Charlie ran up.

"Who in blazes would leave a gate lying down like that?"

"Beats me! I know it was closed when we finished combining last fall. You okay?"

Jimmy rubbed his leg. "Yeah, I think so. Just twisted it a bit." He led Pinto away from the gate while Charlie picked it up and opened it properly, leaning it against the far fence.

Jane had rolled over and was lying on her back making an angel. "So what lop-eared coyote left the gate open?"

"Don't know . . ." Joe retrieved Jimmy's skis and brought them to him. ". . . Country person wouldn't. Not flat across the opening like that."

"Could be a hunter," Jimmy agreed. "Could have been open

since fall. Nobody comes this way to notice. Hurry up Jane!"

Jane got up and put on her skis with deliberate slowness. "I wish to point out," she announced, "that twice today I have fallen because the *people* in front of me have tripped me." She glared at Joe. "If this happens again I am moving up in line!"

They set out again, across the smooth, fresh snow. Now Diamond no longer followed behind the others but turned so that Pinto's skiers took the east side of the field and Diamond's the west. Going in opposite directions meant there would be no risk of accident if one group fell.

The horses galloped and Julie could no longer afford to do anything but watch her skis and hang on. They had completed the length of the field and Julie was bracing herself for the turn when Mary called, "Great going, team. No falls yet!"

It was not looking up at Mary that caused her to stiffen. It was what she saw beyond the fence.

She had known the deserted farm buildings of the old Tyler place ever since she was a little girl. Will used to store grain in the old house before he got the new steel storage bins, and the Morgan children had all explored the place from time to time until the house became so ramshackle that Will declared it too dangerous.

Now, on this bright winter day, Julie felt a sudden lurch of fear, as though the weathered old house, the barn with its sagging roof and empty loft, had something ominous about them. But even that was not what caused her to jerk her head back for another look as they rounded the corner of the field.

It was the smoke.

Chapter Four

Smoke? It couldn't be.

Julie looked back. The next thing she knew, she was down, sprawling in the snow. She got up quickly and stood, staring down at the old Tyler farm. The sagging buildings blended into the hillside as if they had grown there. They had always seemed that way to her. Natural. Like a rock or a tree, part of the landscape. All her life they had been there.

Julie could see the untouched snow piled against the sagging doors, the crumbling brick chimney cold and still against the hillside. But the wisp of smoke she had glimpsed had come, not from the house, but from the old barn.

She skied up to where the others waited patiently, picked up the rope, and braced herself as Diamond trotted away. It could have been a skiff of snow on the roof drifting up at just the moment she had looked, she thought. Somehow she took little comfort in the possibility. The day was calm. Around her the snow lay still in the bright sunshine.

She realized that she would have accepted a glimpse of smoke coming from the roof of the house. As if she had somehow tuned into some long ago whiff of smoke from the time the house had been lived in—had lived. All her life she'd had glimpses of the past.

They circled and cut across the field, and Julie could see the Tyler place again. She used to like to explore the old house, remembered the mouse-smell from warm summer days with Billy, Jane, and Joe. Remembered the fun of discovering broken dishes, old catalogues, a doll's teapot. Why did she feel that more than the ghosts of long departed animals haunted the barn? She sensed pain and something else, something she could not, or did not want to identify.

First the dalmation and now this. She had not changed. For the first time in months she relaxed. Funny how being puzzled about something she should not have seen could do that. But then it was a familiar feeling. All her life she had sensed and seen things. There had always been images and smells she could not interpret, like a kaleidoscope of meaningless messages flashing through her mind. Now it had begun again. But it was better than the blank emptiness of the past few months.

This time she concentrated on making the turn. Across the field she could see Joe wipe out and Jane let go the rope and go swooping off, arms flailing before she too collapsed.

"Jimmy's letting Pinto go too fast." There was concern in Mary's voice.

Charlie laughed. "Never mind! As long as those two clowns aren't complaining."

"Jane would rather spend the day up to her neck in snow than ask anybody to slow down!" Billy really admired his daredevil sister. Their mother had always said, "Jane, if you keep this up, you'll never live to be thirteen!," but she had—that very month.

Mary laughed, "She'll never live to be fourteen!"

"How about you two?" Charlie asked. "Are you about ready to pack it in?"

Julie hoped Billy would say yes but she knew he wouldn't, and so she was grateful when Mary answered for them. "It'll take nearly half an hour to get home. Let's set an example. Besides, Jane's starting to look like an abominable snowman!"

"Mum won't like it if she catches cold." Julie felt it was safe to comment at this point.

A look of understanding passed between Mary and Charlie. "Right!" he said. "Let's set an example!"

Diamond soon realized they were on the way home to barn and hay and set off at a good clip.

Alice Morgan watched from the kitchen window as the two lines of skiers sedately entered the yard. It had been quiet while they were gone. Everything was ready, turkey in the oven, pies lined up on the counter. She'd actually had some time to sit and talk to Will. She was still worried about him, noticed the stiffness in his walk although he denied having any pain. It was good having Charlie home. Will could rest more and the doctor said that was all that was needed.

She opened the door and handed Mary the broom. "Sweep your sister! Jane, you look as though you've brought half the field back on your clothes!"

Jane didn't seem concerned. "Guess who got to ski back AHEAD of Joe!"

Later, as Charlie helped himself to more stuffing and gravy, he remembered and turned to Will. "By the way, the gate to the east quarter was open. Down, just lying on the ground."

"Yeah," added Jimmy, "I caught my ski on it, nearly broke my neck." He noticed his mother's look and amended, "... twisted my ankle ... a little, not much ... it's all right now," he finished quickly.

"Could be hunters?"

"Yeah, could be. Could be something else." Will took a bite of turkey and chewed thoughtfully.

"Billy, you have to eat one vegetable, even at Christmas!" Alice held a bowl of Brussels sprouts out to him and turned to look at her husband. "What do you mean, Will?"

"Paddy Behan told me the other day he lost two head of his young Herefords last fall. One was a calf, just disappeared ... so there's no telling what happened to it. The other though, a yearling steer, he found butchered."

"Butchered?" said Alice incredulously.

"Sort of anyway. Looked like somebody started to cut it up and then just left it to rot. Paddy reported it to the Mounties and Sgt. Pearson came out. Said it was the first case of rustling he's seen in these parts."

"Rustlers!" breathed Joe. "You mean, rootin' tootin' old-time cowboy-type rustlers?"

"I reckon, you and me better saddle up and git them varmints!" from Jimmy.

"Count me in, pardner!" Jane waved her fork fiercely. "The Morgan posse rides tonight!"

"Jane! Put that fork down before you put out someone's eye," Alice spoke absent-mindedly, her attention focused on her husband. "Why didn't Paddy Behan say something to me?"

Will shook his head. "He didn't want to worry you. You had quite a bit on your mind last fall, remember?"

"Rustlers, wow!"

"Not like you think, Billy!" Will shook his head. "No Wild West stuff. Just people in pick-ups or vans, go in and butcher an animal, load it up, and take it back to the city or wherever they came from. Unless they're caught in the act, they can just say they're hunting."

"That's disgraceful!" Alice said. "It's the same as car theft or anything else. Can't the Mounties do anything?"

"Pretty hard. Best they can get is tire tracks, and they could come from miles away. Pearson told Paddy that over a thousand head were rustled that way in Alberta last year alone!"

"Wow," breathed Jimmy, "that amounts to a lot of money."

"I heard about that in one of my courses," put in Charlie. "They said it was something like a million dollars a year because sometimes really valuable purebred breeding stock are butchered. Even when it's just a range-fed butcher steer, you're looking at eight hundred bucks a piece. For the ranchers in the south of the province it's pretty serious."

Alice shook her head. "We haven't lost any, have we?"

"Nope. I had Jimmy ride out and do a count last week when Paddy told me. Our stock's probably too handy to the house and road for anything like that."

"We'd better keep our eyes peeled just the same. I think it's shocking that people can get away with such a thing!" Alice glanced around the table, her expression softening as she looked at her family. "Billy! One Brussels sprout does not count as enough vegetable for a meal!"

"Even at Christmas?" Billy looked hopefully at his mother.

Alice laughed, "Maybe at Christmas!"

Julie climbed into bed that night and sat gazing at the china dalmation. It had been a nice Christmas even if the peace she had known in the last months was gone. But then so was the uncertainty.

Now there were other uncertainties. She remembered the wisp of smoke. The old barn, dark and ominous in the sparkling sunlit snow. She shivered and snuggled down beneath the new down-filled comforter.

She had not wanted her mother to replace her old quilt but Alice Morgan had insisted. "At least for the winter, Julie, you need something warmer. Besides this quilt is practically an antique. Some of the patches that went into it are from clothes almost a hundred years old."

Julie knew that better than anyone. The worn blue satin patch had been from her great-grandmother Morgan's wedding gown. Sometimes when she had rubbed the patch she could see great-Granny Morgan but that too had stopped after the accident.

She wondered now if it would be different. If things had changed back. Like the dalmation.

Like the smoke?

Rustlers, Will had said. Julie shut her eyes. She could see the old buildings, the barn with its wisp of smoke frozen in her memory of this afternoon. And Death inside the barn. The calf? Julie had felt the deaths of animals before. Long ago buffalo plummeting to their deaths, even chickens that would end up as dinner. This was different. This made her shiver under the warm comforter. She sat up. She had to clear her mind, tear it away from the sense of foreboding that had seemed to envelop the Tyler barn.

She got up and carefully lifted the dalmation from its little stand on the shelf and held it to her cheek. The warmth was soothing. She carried it back to bed with her, laying it gently beside her pillow. Gradually she relaxed. It was as if all the fresh air and exercise had taken the tension from her body. Even her bones seemed limp. It was a lovely feeling. Peaceful. She slept.

Chapter Five

Julie had never paid much attention to the fact that she sometimes knew what people were thinking. It hadn't been a problem. She remembered teachers looking at her strangely when she'd answered a question on something they hadn't studied. She had wondered herself why the answer popped into her head with such clarity as the teacher stared at her, waiting. She'd solved the problem by not raising her eyes. She had the reputation of being shy anyway.

But after Christmas messages sometimes flashed into her mind. Silly things, that made no sense. Once or twice she had answered a question from Billy or Jane, and they'd said, "That's funny, I was just going to ask you that!" and Julie realized they hadn't spoken.

Trouble came during the Easter tests. Julie was stuck on the last Social Studies question. She was staring across the rows at Susan Brown. Their gazes locked for a moment, then Susan gave her a quick relieved smile and the answer popped into Julie's head. It was not until the next morning when Miss Friesen kept Susan and Julie in at recess for a lecture on cheating that Julie realized what had happened.

"I know you two were sitting rows apart, but it's very peculiar when the only two students who answer a question correctly use precisely the same phrasing in that answer." Miss Friesen stared at them, but Julie kept her eyes on her desk. "Did you study together?"

Julie and Susan were not friends, not enemies either, but Susan was a popular, outgoing person, always surrounded by other girls, the centre of the Grade 5 activities. And Julie had always been a loner. She liked it that way, even though it meant that sometimes when they had to pair up for something she got stuck with a boy, usually Simon Dueck.

Simon wasn't very popular. In the lower grades they'd called him "Simple Simon" but the last few years he'd had the highest marks in class so the joke wore out. He wasn't good at sports and the boys at Hurry Elementary were keen on soccer, every recess and noon, so Simon was a loner too.

The other kids had teased Julie and Simon at first but when they figured out neither of them cared it died down.

Once in a while when one of the girls was away sick Julie paired up with a girl, but never Susan. Susan was so popular, she was always the first one teamed up.

Now, Julie could feel Miss Friesen's eyes fixed on her but she didn't dare look up. She didn't know how to answer.

"I've never seen you two studying together. . . ."

Julie realized Miss Friesen was giving them an out. But she still couldn't think of anything to say.

Luckily Susan could. "You see, we ride the same school bus. Sometimes we sit together."

Julie was overcome with admiration for Susan's quick thinking. It was the sort of answer Jane would have come up with. Not exactly a lie. In fact Susan hadn't lied at all. They did ride the same bus and once or twice, when the weather was really cold and the few kids who were riding that day crowded up at the front, Susan had come and sat beside Julie.

She waited for Miss Friesen to ask another question. Almost against her will she looked up and sensed the teacher's relief. The puzzle had been solved to her satisfaction.

"I didn't think either of you girls would stoop to cheating. Thank you for explaining things." Miss Friesen smiled and went to her desk.

Out in the hall, Susan breathed a sigh of relief. "Well, she may be satisfied, but I'm still wondering how we did it!"

Julie wished Susan would just forget the whole thing. "I guess it was just a coincidence."

"Hey!" Susan stopped suddenly. "Maybe we've got E.S.P.!"

Julie wanted to keep on walking to the door, to the safety

of the crush of kids outside, the recess hubbub.

"E.S.P.?" She stopped reluctantly and turned to Susan.

"Yeah! I forget what the letters stand for. You know, sort of mind reading."

Julie yearned to escape. Just a few more yards to the door and she would be outside, where a knot of Susan's friends were watching and waiting to carry Susan off, away from Julie and this awkward situation.

But Susan's hands were on her shoulders pulling her face to face. "Let's try it. I'll think of something . . . something I've never told anybody and you try to read my mind. . . . Ummm . . . let's see . . ."

Julie fought the impulse to pull away and run. She used to wish that popular girls like Susan would pay more attention to her, but now all she wanted was the old, safe anonymity. Still, it would look strange if she refused. Susan was just being friendly, offering Julie the attention she gave her friends. Julie tried to relax.

"Okay, I've got it. Look into my eyes and I'll concentrate!"

Fascinated, Julie looked. She knew she should say something, anything, to break this. But she couldn't resist. She decided that if it worked and she really did get some sort of message from Susan she'd just say something ordinary that would convince Susan there wasn't any E.S.P. going on.

Susan's eyes were riveted to Julie's. The message was loud and clear in Julie's head. In the shock of how definite it was and what a surprise it was Julie almost forgot herself and blurted it out. "You've got a *crush* on Billy!" As it was, she knew her expression had changed as she stared at Susan wide-eyed with amazement. Frantically she searched her mind for something to say. It had to be something Susan hadn't told anybody, she supposed. And it had to be as far away from Billy and crushes as possible.

"You're going to spend Easter in Edmonton?" Julie said it hesitantly. The Browns didn't have any relatives in Edmonton that she had ever heard of. It would be wrong, and it would be so far from what Susan was thinking that she would be off the hook. Julie sighed with relief.

Susan looked crestfallen. "I wish you were right!" She laughed. "At least I don't have to worry about you finding out my innermost thoughts!"

Julie started to turn, but Susan held on to her shoulders.

"My turn now! You think of something and I'll try to guess it." She stared into Julie's eyes.

Even though she was sure there wasn't much chance of Susan really being able to read her mind, Julie tried to clear her thoughts of anything to do with what had gone before. Her mind was in turmoil and the predominant thought just now was the shock of how easy it was to read minds. At least if the person focused and looked into her eyes. Frantically she thought of math problems, puppies, anything to concentrate on. She finally settled for the nine times table. It wouldn't hurt to practice.

Susan stared for a minute and then shook her head and laughed. "What you're probably thinking is that if we don't get going we'll miss the whole recess!"

Julie smiled at Susan with relief. "That wasn't it, but it may have crossed my mind. Let's go."

They went through the door companionably, the anxious faces of Susan's friends read the good news, and she was soon the centre of attention.

Julie stood quietly on the fringe of the group waiting for the end-of-recess buzzer to go. One of the things she had learned in her lifetime of coping with strange things was to control her face. It was expressionless but inside she was a flurry of emotions. Excitement and fear predominated. By the time the buzzer went she had calmed down enough to tell herself nothing had really changed. She wasn't even sure the message about Billy was right, though she couldn't think why such a thing would have occurred to her.

Ever since Christmas she felt as if she'd opened Pandora's Box. Except instead of nasty moths representing the evils of the world, Julie had unleashed thoughts. Thoughts that only confused her.

Sometimes she wished she'd never tried anything, never even thought of trying anything. There was no question in her mind that she could, by concentrating, tune into other people's thoughts. But usually it was just a confusing, senseless jumble. As if a radio wasn't set on the station properly and was getting more than one station. It only seemed to work when Julie was alone with someone, looking into their eyes. She had tried it at home now and then but it was too conspicuous.

"Mum!" Jane would yell. "Julie's staring at me with those moo-cow eyes again!" And then Jane would cross her eyes and make faces and make Julie giggle. Once, when she had tried it on her mother, Alice had simply looked concerned, felt Julie's forehead, and sent her to bed. She'd had better luck with her father, but all she could read in Will's eyes was affection and some amusement at the way she was looking at him. Billy had been hopeless. He never seemed to settle down long enough to look at anything. Let alone into anything.

She remembered that it was Thursday, which meant that the Morgans didn't have to take the bus home. Their mother did her shopping that afternoon and always picked them up after school. Good. She could slip down to the library and find out what E.S.P. meant. It would be wonderful to know. Maybe there would even be some information about other people and how they handled it.

Chapter Six

The Hurry Elementary and Junior High School Library doubled as the town library and stayed open to the public Thursday and Friday evenings, but usually after school there would be nobody there but Miss Johnson.

Ada Johnson had been librarian at Hurry School as long as Julie could remember. Before that she'd been a teacher. She had even taught Will Morgan when he was a boy.

"Johnson's due to retire," Julie had heard one of the teachers mumble one day when she'd had some of her students restricted from the library for bad behaviour. But students like Julie, who loved to read, were quietly devoted to Miss Johnson. Julie especially liked to come in Thursday afternoons after the bell when there would be nobody there but Miss Johnson.

But today she was worried. She wasn't sure how to approach the subject of E.S.P. Miss Johnson had the reputation of being preoccupied and easily distracted. And yet she had, in the past, startled Julie with shrewd questions and comments when they were least expected. Would she want to know why Julie was interested in E.S.P.? She was not one of those teachers who could be put off by evasive answers.

Julie was relieved to find the library empty when she arrived. It gave her time. She sat, letting the peaceful feel of the room sink into her bones, the late afternoon sunshine coming through the window, Miss Johnson's pet African violets lining the sill. The velvety purple, blue, and pink blooms brightened the room, but Julie didn't like the fuzzy leaves or the juicy stems that snapped and bled if you so much as touched them.

She loved the rows and rows of friendly books. The old ones

were best. Ones without garish book jackets, the old cloth covers blending in soft browns and greens and blues, faded with age. When she held them or even as she sat there looking at them she could sense the trees they came from. As if there was something of Nature still in the heart of them.

"Were you waiting for me, Julie?"

Julie was startled by the voice. She looked up into Miss Johnson's face. It was an interesting face. Marked with many things Julie didn't understand. Like a map of living, or a history drawn in skin. Not like the younger teachers whose smooth faces told no secrets, betrayed no past. It wasn't blank. Almost reluctantly Julie looked into Miss Johnson's eyes. And was swept away by something sad. So sad that she quickly looked down, remembered the question, and mumbled, ". . . Ummm, no . . ." She wasn't sure how to approach the subject. ". . . I was just . . ."

She didn't have to finish. There was the clomp of heels in the hall and Mabel Piggott swept into the library like a tidal wave.

"Well, Miss Johnson!" she boomed. Her voice seemed to bounce off the walls, the ceiling, and trickle into every cranny of the room.

Julie actually tightened her grip on the desk to avoid being swept away. Even Miss Johnson seemed to be holding herself steady against the onslaught. "Have you got my books in yet?" It was an accusation, as if Miss Johnson deliberately, wilfully, prevented the books from coming.

Miss Johnson turned toward her desk. "As a matter of fact the inter-library loan books arrived today, Mrs. Piggott. One of the books you ordered is still unavailable, but the rest are here."

"Unavailable! What do you mean 'unavailable'? Where do our tax dollars go anyway? It really is disgraceful that this library doesn't stock a few books on the paranormal. I resent having to order every book I want."

"There really isn't much demand, you see . . ." began Miss Johnson.

"Of course not! Backwoods libraries, backwoods people.

Someone needs to take them in hand. Naturally people don't borrow books they can't find."

"The inter-library loan service works quite well. We got every one of those books you ordered on U.F.O.'s right away."

"The material was positively ancient history. And I'm past that outer-space nonsense anyway." Mrs Piggott tapped her forehead significantly. "Inner space!" she boomed. "That's where it's at. The Mind. The Human Brain. It's the last frontier! The fools explore the moon and we know nothing about the possibilities of our own minds." She pounded over to the desk, almost knocking over a small display table as she did so. "I hope you've done better this time. I'm particularly interested in reading about the experiments they've done on E.S.P. in the Soviet Union." Julie watched as Mrs Piggott slammed the books down one by one. "Of course, it would be the one I'm most anxious to read!"

"It should be in next week." Miss Johnson began to stamp the books.

Mrs Piggott produced her library card and a list. "You'd better send for these now . . . since I only get half the books I order!"

Miss Johnson took the list and the card and continued to stamp.

"Extra Sensory Perception! That's the solution to everything. What would we need with technology if we could transmit our thoughts? Language barriers would cease to exist. Boundaries would be as nothing. It could mean world peace. We just need to develop the amazing powers of the human brain." Mrs Piggott leaned over the desk snatching the books from Miss Johnson's hand. "You know, I think I've got it!" Not waiting for a reply she left, storming down the hall, leaving Julie feeling very much like a battered beach after the wave swept out.

Miss Johnson straightened and set her chin firmly. "That woman!" she said.

Julie got up. She could see her mother's car pulling into the parking lot. If she left quickly Miss Johnson might not even ask her why she'd been waiting in the library.

Miss Johnson was still staring after Mabel Piggott, her smile tight. "I once read that hell is a place where you know what

26

other people are thinking of you!" she said. "Good night, Julie."

The look in Miss Johnson's eyes was not amused.

"Good night, Miss Johnson." Julie hurried down the hall. Miss Johnson's thoughts had been loud and clear, and it was lucky for Mabel Piggott that she didn't have E.S.P.

Outside, the battered Piggott Oldsmobile was already speeding towards the highway as Julie squeezed in the back seat between Billy and Joe.

"Almost an accident out here a minute ago, Julie!" Billy informed her.

"Yeah," put in Jane, "Piggott nearly got the number 6 bus this time." There was a pause as they all looked at their mother, waiting.

"Did you have a bad day, Mum?" Billy asked when there was no response.

Alice seemed to rouse herself. "No. Why do you ask?"

"Jane called Mrs. Piggott, 'Piggott' and you didn't bawl her out."

"Jane, how many times . . ." Alice began, then noticing their expectant faces, just laughed and shook her head.

Julie settled back into the seat, not listening to the others.

So E.S.P. stood for Extra Sensory Perception. Not necessarily mind-reading as Susan had said. Extra Sensory Perception. She said it over in her head. It seemed right somehow. Not just the meaning but the way the words flowed. Sometimes words did that. It sounded dignified and special. She decided that if she had to be labelled, this was definitely better than just plain weird.

Chapter Seven

Easter Monday morning Julie climbed crocus hill with Mary. The great dome of prairie sky overhead with its constantly shifting clouds usually filled her with pleasure, as if her spirits could rise to fill the space. But today she felt ill at ease. She wasn't sure why.

The ritual of searching for the first crocus flowers was something they had done here every year since Julie could remember. She'd named the hill when she was little and the name had stuck.

Easter was late this year, but there were still patches of snow on the northern faces of hills and along the fence lines, tucked against the shrubs in ditches. On the hill the grass was still dry and dead, but Julie could see the first clump of purple flowers.

"They're here!" she called. Suddenly her foreboding was forgotten and she was running, throwing herself on the ground beside them. She loved the fuzzy purple flowers blooming in the midst of the dry grass, defying the chill nights, the still-frozen ground.

She lay there drinking in their specialness—their newness. They were the first sign of life in the dead-grass, winter-beaten world.

Mary came and sat beside her. "So what do you want from this new year?"

Julie couldn't remember when they had started this. This special wish. But she knew that somehow New Year's Day had always seemed to her an artificial way to start the year. For her the new year began now and here, with the first crocus.

Oh, sometimes she joined Jane wishing on the evening star,

"Star light, star bright,
first star I see tonight,
wish I may, wish I might,
have the wish I wish tonight."

but she would wish for little things: a good mark on a test the next day, a chance to go to Red Deer with her father the next time he went, that nobody would remember it was her turn to do dishes, things like that.

This was different. This was a once-a-year wish. Special and not to be wasted. She didn't hesitate.

"For Daddy to be really, really better. As if the accident had never happened," she said.

Mary nodded, "That's good, Julie. A good wish. I'm going to be more selfish. I'm going to wish that I get a summer job that pays enough so that I can pay my own fees in the fall."

Julie knew that Mary was worrying about leaving to take nursing in Edmonton in the fall. Their parents hadn't said anything but the message at Christmas had been loud and clear. So were the conversations they overheard whenever farmers got together. Low sale prices on feeder cattle, higher and higher prices if you had to buy feed, and out-of-sight interest on loans for equipment. There was a lot of head shaking. Every farm child knew the meaning of the words "cash flow." When money came in only when grain or stock was sold, maybe once or twice a year, ready money was hard to find. And a thousand dollars for university fees times two children could be a major problem.

They sat for a while. Julie watched a tiny insect crawl down the inside of the petal. She wondered where it had come from, how it had appeared just at the moment the crocus did. Suddenly, with a feeling that was almost pain it was so sharp, she was filled with envy. How wondrous it would be to be walking in the midst of that gentle purple beauty. Enveloped and safe. Was this the lot of a tiny, insignificant bug? To live its short life in surroundings more beautiful than any fairy-tale princess? Living a dream Julie could only imagine in a velvet crocus palace. Never knowing that it was really just an ugly little black bug. What does it think? she wondered. Does it dream great dreams of the world outside? Does it remember the dead grass, the frozen ground? Winter?

Julie shivered a little. The sun had seemed so bright and the day so spring-like that she had just pulled on an extra sweater. Now she wished she had brought her parka the way Mary had told her to. She looked around. She had been so engrossed she had not noticed Mary leave. She was probably on the western slope of the hill looking for more crocuses. Julie stood up. She couldn't see Mary but wasn't concerned. She was probably over the brow of the hill.

Julie's legs were stiff from sitting on the cold ground. Not only that but she felt a little dizzy. It reminded her of times when she was little, when she used to squat by puddles, head down, watching water bugs, building little islands and bridges for them. Sometimes she sat bent over so long in those days that she would have to stand still a long time before her head quit spinning.

She must have been sitting a long time. The sky was unfriendly now, heavy with clouds. That was why she'd grown cold. Without the sun's warmth it cooled off quickly. Will had once told her that his Granny Morgan could smell bad weather coming. Was that why she had felt uneasy when she first arrived?

She crested the hill and stood alone beneath the turbulent sky. Below her the old buildings of the Tyler place stood cold and alone, the remnants of drifted snow pressed against the house and barn.

She recalled Christmas day and shivered, remembering the smoke. She could not believe that it was the weather alone that disturbed her now.

She was still standing transfixed, staring at the old barn, when Mary called her. She pulled herself away with difficulty as if the buildings held her in some sort of trance. Walking away, each step was an effort and a release as well. As she started down the hill on the other side she felt as if a band holding her snapped and she knew without looking back that the buildings were no longer in sight.

Mary was waiting, looking anxiously at the sky and, as Julie began to run toward her, she felt the first drop of rain. That was all they needed—to be cold and wet. By the time Julie caught up with Mary it was coming down steadily. It would take them half an hour to get home, less if they ran but they would be soaked.

"I wish I'd made you bring your parka," Mary said ruefully. Julie noticed that she hadn't brought hers either. "At least it's not snowing."

"It might be better if it was. At least we wouldn't get as wet." Even as Julie spoke she realized the rain was changing to snow. Not gentle flakes but sharp granules that stung when they hit her face. They were walking fast, not quite running, and Julie should have felt warmer but she seemed to be shivering just as much.

The sky no longer showed its clouds, just a blanket of grey pressing down on them as the snow grew thicker with each passing moment.

Mary stopped. "It's no use. It's too far. If the snow gets any heavier, we won't be able to see where we're going in another few minutes."

Already the trees along the fence line not far from them were blurred, and the horizons had long since disappeared into the greyness behind the whirling snow.

Julie felt herself turned around, pulled almost off balance, as Mary abruptly headed back the way they had come. "We can shelter at the old Tyler place. Maybe even get a fire going. At least we'll be out of the wind until the snow lets up."

Reluctantly, Julie allowed herself to be pulled along. The feeling of dread that had held her staring down at the buildings came back as they climbed the hill. She knew they were at the top even before she felt the ground start to slope down beneath her feet.

The snow was fat flakes now, whirling this way and that, pulled by the gusts of wind, now dropping in a calm, now blown horizontally, sometimes drifting upwards for a moment. It was all they could see. They could not make out the buildings below.

Julie stared up, at the snowflakes whirlpooling down. There

was something hypnotic about them that held her eyes. As they walked she had the feeling they were being sucked into something. Something cold and still. And she couldn't stop shivering.

Chapter Eight

"If we keep going straight down, we'll hit the fence. Then we can follow it until we're close enough to see the house."

Mary looked down. She had her arm around Julie and could feel her shivering. At least I *hope* we can see the house, she thought, it's not that close to the fence. She gave Julie an extra squeeze. The kid's nearly frozen but she's not complaining, just plodding along. I've got to get her out of this, it's my fault for not making her bring her parka. And what an idiot not to bring mine.

Walking was slower now. Being that close together made it awkward. As well the slope of the hill had sharpened, which made it harder to walk on the uneven ground. They could hardly see their feet, let alone the ground beneath in the swirling, drifting snow. Mary could feel her stomach tense. They'd never be able to see the house from the fence.

And then there it was. The fence. They almost walked into it. It was only an arm's length in front of them before the barbed wire showed. Without a word, she put her foot on the bottom wire to hold it down and lifted the wire above so that Julie could crawl through without catching her sweater.

When she was through, Mary wanted to walk in front but decided against it. Side by side, between Julie and the fence, she could keep an eye on both as they moved along in the direction the house would be. Now they were able to tuck their freezing hands in their sweater sleeves.

Concentrate, Mary thought, as she peered into the swirling snow. We mustn't miss the house. Mary remembered summers and summers of play here. The place was as familiar as her own yard. Surely she could find a landmark. The lilac bushes between the house and the fence would be the best bet. If only she could see them.

"Watch for the lilac bushes, Julie," she called, but the wind caught her words, even her breath, and swept them away so that she could hardly hear her own voice. Head down, Julie plodded steadily, oblivious. Mary considered reaching out and tapping her and yelling in her ear, but it seemed too much effort.

She pushed her wet, snowy hair out of her face and peered into the swirling snow. Fence to the left, house to the right. How far? How far had they come? They weren't moving very fast. She remembered bright, sun-warm days, racing along the fence. Only seconds, it seemed, to get to the house. How long had they been walking? Not long, they were going so slow.

Mary stumbled over something. She remembered one of those summer days. Joe and Jimmy, six and eight then, deciding to build a stone fort beside the fence. They gave up after hauling about half a dozen rocks. But the stones had stayed by the fence, almost in line with the lilacs and the house. She grabbed Julie and turned her so that they stood at right angles to the fence.

"Okay, Julie!" she yelled. "If we walk in a straight line we'll hit the house!"

As Mary pushed her face against her sister's ear she could feel Julie's hair, not just wet but stiff with snow. It was freezing. They were freezing.

"We've got to hit the house," she added under her breath. The temperature was dropping and they had to get out of the storm soon. She held Julie by the shoulders, pushing her ahead. "Take giant steps!" she yelled. "That way we're more likely to walk in a straight line." Mary did not want to think what would happen if they veered off course and missed the house. They could wander for hours and they did not have hours. They were too cold already.

She remembered warm spring days of hide and seek, hiding in the lilacs, the thick, sweet scent of their blooming all around her. Purple clusters overhead blotted out the sky. Six bounds and she could reach the house, sidle around, and touch the front door that was home base.

She pulled Julie back and took her hand. She had to concentrate, judge the straightness and the distance. Two giant steps. One more and she should see the bushes on the left and know she was on course. Yes, there they were, some branches caught on her sweater. Good. They were close and moving straight. Now, six more. Mary counted under her breath, "four, five . . ." Thump! Her outstretched arm hit the wall of the house. She wanted to laugh hysterically. Only five steps now, she thought, I'm bigger.

She leaned against the wall, catching her breath a moment, hugging Julie against her. Now to get inside. Shelter was just around the corner.

The full brunt of the wind and snow hit them as they edged around the house, but Mary, leading the way, didn't care. There was the old door. She slapped its icy surface. "Home Free!" she breathed triumphantly.

Maybe she could even make a fire in the old cast iron stove. In spite of the cold, she was feeling exultant as she pulled to open the door.

Her triumph died instantly. The door was solid. Unmoving.

Julie shook her head and tugged at Mary's arm. "It's nailed," she screamed over the wind. "The other door is too. Daddy nailed them after the floor caved in."

Mary remembered now. Remembered the conversation between her parents. Alice insisting, "We don't want someone going in, falling in the cellar . . . injured and we might not get there until too late."

The wind biting at her face, Mary remembered the words. ". . . not get there until too late." She stared at the door, hopelessness welling up within her. Even in despair she knew better than to waste her strength trying to break it down. Even with tools, with hands that weren't half frozen, she doubted that she and Julie could break in.

Chapter Nine

Julie was shivering violently as they huddled together against the door. It was the worst possible place to be, she thought. They were completely exposed to the wind and there was no porch. Even the door-frame had been covered over by the tightly nailed boards.

Mary put her face close to Julie's ear and yelled. "I don't think it's safe to head for the barn. It's a long way, and if we miss it . . ." If they missed it there was a quarter section of land to wander in—bush along the fence line at the road allowance half a mile away—but they would never make it. Mary held Julie tight trying to shelter her from the wind. "And yet . . . it's our only chance . . . we've got to get out of the storm. Oh, Julie," Mary slumped against the door, "I'm sorry. . . . I should have made you wear your parka or gone back sooner or . . ."

Somehow in the midst of the cold and fear, Julie felt a tinge of amazement. Mary was giving up! It couldn't be! Mary never panicked, never quit. Julie stared at her. She shook her head, "No." It was just the soundless forming of her lips but the word screamed in her head. No! Mary could not give up and No! they could not stay there and louder than all the others No! Julie did not want to face their only option—the barn.

With a crooked smile Mary squared her shoulders, "Come on, Julie. We can't stay here. Let's give it our best shot!" She pushed Julie away from the door, walking straight into the stinging wind.

Julie felt herself held by the shoulders and pushed forward. The snow whirled and clawed at her. She knew the tears were freezing on her face. She couldn't feel her cheeks anymore but didn't want to pull her hands from her sleeves even for a minute. With each step the barn and shelter were closer. And what else? With each step the dread grew, welling up, blocking out the senses—the chill of her wet clothes, the biting wind, the tiredness.

She let Mary push her, almost let herself be pushed on past the barn, although she knew without any doubt exactly where it was and could have walked straight to it, even though there was no sign of it, not shape nor shadow to give it away in the storm.

She felt herself pulled to a halt. Mary turning her and pulling her close, yelling in her ear. For a minute Julie did not even pay attention to the words, so great was her relief at the respite from dread, the comforting warmth of being held by her sister. But the words were there and true.

"It's no use, Julie. We should have been there by now, unless we're walking in a circle, and I don't think we are. We've got to try to get back to the house . . . find something, boards . . . something to make a windbreak . . ."

It was the despair on Mary's face or the white streaks on her cheeks, snow-tracked with tears, that finally broke through to Julie. That made her turn despite the dread, the fear she could not understand, and walk, pulling Mary behind her, straight toward the looming shape she knew and felt before she saw it. The barn.

They hit the southeast corner, moved along quickly now. Mary leading, almost running as she pulled Julie toward the small south door. They both knew the big sliding doors for the livestock had been lifted off the tracks and nailed down and that the only way in were the little doors on the north and south.

There was no old snow against the door but the storm had already piled a small drift against it. Luckily the newly drifted snow was soft and pushed away easily as Mary undid the hook and shoved Julie inside.

For a minute Julie felt nothing. Only her sister's arms around her and Mary jumping up and down. "We did it! We made it! I thought we were goners." Mary pulled Julie around in a crazy stumbling dance.

Julie felt like a rag doll, flipped this way and that by her owner. How could Mary be so happy? Couldn't she feel it? Feel the pressure of horror lurking around them?

"We can make it now. We're going to be okay! In a few hours the storm will stop and Dad and Charlie will come for us. They'll probably come here first thing too. . . . Mum knew we were going to look for crocuses on the hill . . . and they'll know we'd come here when the storm started." Mary was laughing and crying at once.

Their drunken dance had warmed Julie a little but she still clung to her sister. Mary was safe in here. Julie tried to hold onto that. For herself she wasn't sure. The storm had been less frightening than the fear and dread the barn held for her.

The storm had darkened the day, but inside the barn had always been gloomy. Even when she was little Julie remembered refusing to come in here, but it had not been the same, not as intense. She wondered if the barn had changed, or if the change was somehow in herself. Some sensitivity that had awakened and grown after last year.

Mary was still hugging her, just rocking back and forth. "To think, Julie, I used to hate this barn when I was a kid. It was so dark and gloomy with most of the windows all boarded up. The boys always wanted to play hide and seek in here . . . before Dad took all the stalls out so he could store machinery there were a million places to hide . . . or jump out and scare your sister, which was probably the whole point of it, now that I think about it. Anyway, I hated it, although it was fun swinging on the rafters. Jimmy even had a bunch of ropes, so he could pretend to be Tarzan swinging through the jungle. Until he missed a vine one day and broke his leg and Dad made us take them down."

Mary looked around smiling. "Well, I don't hate the old place anymore, Julie. It's going to save our lives." Mary paused. "At least it will, if I can get you to stop shivering. You're shaking like a leaf! If only I had some matches, we could build a fire." She felt in her pocket and came up with a Kleenex and wiped Julie's wet face. "Not much use, it's too damp."

Julie realized that Mary's sweater came only to her waist,

unlike the one Julie had on, one of Jane's old ones, that hung down almost to her knees. And she was wearing a sweater underneath too. Mary was wearing only that one short sweater. At least they were both wearing wool. She remembered reading somewhere that wool, even when wet, was a good insulator. Still, Mary must be a lot colder. Her face was wet too.

Julie reached under her sweater to see if she had a Kleenex in her pocket. No, she'd forgotten as usual, but she had something better. She held a triumphant hand out to Mary.

"Matches! Julie! That's right, you got stuck with burning the garbage for Mum just before we left this morning." Mary held Julie a moment before she took them.

Chapter Ten

"**Q**uick! Julie, there must be some old boards, leftover pieces of stalls or mangers . . . there's a pile of stuff over here." Mary was off, plunging towards the northeast corner that was dimly lit by the ventilator shaft far above.

Julie stood alone, frozen to the spot, feeling the fear press in on her. Her hand raised as if to hold her sister back but unable to move.

Mercifully, Mary was back, dropping an armful of boards, dragging a longer plank, the nails still in it. In her presence, the pressure on Julie seemed to ease a little and Julie moved toward her.

"Pile these up . . . I've got to find some smaller bits, or straw or something to catch the flame." And Mary was gone again, leaving Julie alone. She bent towards the boards. A gesture of cringing, almost an effort to hide behind them. As if she could make herself small enough to escape. So great was her concentration that she barely heard Mary's cry of triumph.

"Paper! Somebody's left some magazines here!" Mary came back carrying two torn magazines she had found in the dark against the far wall. "Funny, I didn't know anybody came here other than us . . ." Mary's face contorted as she came into the light and leafed through the pages. "Oh sick! Whoever . . . ?" She began tearing pages, crumpling them angrily in disgust. "Who could look at it . . . let alone print it . . . let alone . . . ? Perverts!" She seemed in a frenzy of tearing and did not stop until there was nothing but a pile of scraps and crumpled paper.

Julie moved closer. She needed Mary, wanted to touch her for comfort, for reassurance.

"Don't look!" Mary began to shove the paper under the boards. "You didn't see, did you?" She took Julie by the shoulders, looking into her face.

Julie still couldn't speak, but the touch of Mary's hands seemed to bring her back to life a little. She shook her head.

"Well, don't look, just stay here. I think I saw some smaller bits of wood over there, in the dark, by the north wall."

Again, she left Julie. Again, Julie's hand rose protestingly, as if following her, fluttered weakly, and drew back somehow repelled.

Julie crouched by the boards. She did not want to watch Mary but she forced herself. Somehow it was there, the north wall, that was the most frightening. She would have stopped Mary, had she been able to move, but she couldn't. She could only watch her sister walk towards what Julie knew was the source of the fear she felt. The centre of some evil greater than Julie could imagine.

And then something triggered a memory. A picture in the old *Book of Knowledge*. The one of Joan of Arc at the stake, the flames around her. Julie hated bonfires because she always saw Joan in them. Joan holding a cross that was only two sticks tied together. Like the two sticks that Mary was trying to pry off the north wall right now. Bound together to form a cross like Joan's except . . . except the cross loosely nailed to the barn wall was wrong. It was upside down.

And then she couldn't see Mary anymore. There were flames between them and screaming, terrible screaming, and Julie put her arms over her head and shut her eyes.

When she opened them a second later the barn was in darkness again. Mary had the sticks, and was walking toward her.

"There's been a campfire or something over here. Why don't we bring our boards and paper over and just use the same spot?" She bent to pick up some boards.

Julie spoke for the first time. It was as if she hadn't spoken for years, or as if she had never spoken before in her life. The words seemed to pull her throat apart. "No. . . . NO!" It was almost like a sob but loud, a choking scream. She grabbed for Mary, pulling the boards away, throwing them back down. It

41

took her a moment to react to the look of surprise on her sister's face. "Not there . . . it . . . it's too dark."

Mary stared at her a moment, surprised at her vehemence, and then looked back towards the corner, then shrugged. "Okay, I guess you're right. I'll bring the charred bits of wood over here. They'll catch faster than these boards." Mary turned and was gone, leaving Julie alone, staring after her.

It took Mary three matches to get the fire going. The paper did help. The old boards would never have burned without kindling.

Julie crouched beside it, watching as the flames licked at the old charred wood. When it began to smoulder, she looked away, afraid that somehow the relighting of that old fire would show her things she did not want to see. She could not bear to hear the screaming, or know what had caused it.

Mary came back again and again from the corners, finding bits of board, one large enough to make a sort of bench for them to sit on. Julie let herself be pulled onto it beside her sister. She was shivering uncontrollably now but would not let herself look at, or move closer to the fire.

She marvelled at Mary's delight with their situation. How could she feel so happy here in this place so filled with . . . with . . . and then Julie knew what it was, what part of the horror was. It was Death and it was at the north side of the barn.

"There now that's better isn't it?" Mary gave Julie's shoulder a squeeze. The larger boards were catching fire now and Julie could feel the warmth on her face as she stared intently at her feet determined not to look in the fire. Never before in her life had she wished so much to be "normal." Never to have to fight against seeing and knowing hidden things.

"You should stop shivering soon." Mary shuffled on the makeshift bench. "Just stay here and get warmed up. I saw something over there I want to investigate." Mary jumped up from beside her and was off before Julie could stop her.

She seemed to be gone a long time. And Julie dared, at last, to look in the direction she feared.

Mary was standing, a lighted match in her hand so that Julie could see her face in the flickering light. Whether it was that the storm was letting up and the corner was less dark now or that Julie's eyes had adjusted to the dimly lit barn, Julie didn't know. All she knew was that she could see what Mary saw as if she were looking through Mary's eyes and she wanted Mary to come back to her. Now.

She did. She came to the bench, put her arm around Julie's shaking body, and held her tight. When she spoke her voice was very low. "Don't go over there Julie. It's not nice. It . . . it's . . . why would someone *do* that?" Mary's voice became almost shrill. "I don't understand."

Julie didn't either and what was more she didn't want to. She was doing multiplication tables now. Anything to keep her mind from filling with the sounds and sights she feared. She'd tried nursery rhymes but somehow they just pulled her back to this place and what had happened here. "Little Jack Horner sat in a corner" triggered the darkness, the corner of the barn, the horror of this place.

Mary's voice broke through $7 \times 9 =$. Just as well, Julie thought, I always have trouble with that one and have to subtract 7 from 70.

"I wonder if Dad and Charlie are on their way yet? I'm not sure but I think the storm is letting up a little. I could go peek out the door and see." Mary did not move and Julie knew that she was as reluctant to leave as Julie was to have her go even for a moment.

Julie turned and smiled for the first time since they had entered the barn. It was not meant for reassurance, although Mary assumed it was. It was relief. At last Julie knew how to prevent the terror from filling her mind: she would concentrate on Will and where he was. Was he coming? Did he know where they were?

She thought of the biting wind outside, pictured herself outside, and felt, in spite of the spitting snow, only relief as she distanced herself mentally from the barn and the horror it held.

If Will and Charlie were coming, even on the skidoo, they would probably take the road, the way they had come with the horses on Christmas Day. Crossing the open fields would be too dangerous in the blizzard.

Julie let her mind follow the fence, the old road allowance, then the main road all the way back to the farm. There was no sign of them. She could see the farmhouse clearly, even the skidoo sitting in its usual spot. Perhaps they were waiting for the storm to let up. But the car was gone. Had they taken it?

And then she remembered. Mum had said something about going to Hurry to do some shopping with Mary Behan. Dad might think they had gone with her. She realized with a shudder that nobody knew they were missing.

Chapter Eleven

Will Morgan had been out with the tractor and stack mover getting feed for the cattle when the snow began. It was good to be feeling well again. At first, after the accident, he had been grateful just to be alive but worried too that he would never again be able to lead the active, rugged life of a farmer. How would he support his family? Could Charlie and the other boys handle the work with him only able to supervise? He knew that he didn't worry as much as Alice did. Now that he was almost back to normal it seemed a miracle, something he hadn't dared hope for, and he accepted it with quiet gratitude.

He was an accepting man. Maybe that was why he had never questioned the things his youngest daughter did. Alice had worried so much about Julie when she was little. Why she talked of things she could never have seen, had never been told. It hadn't bothered Will. Partly, he supposed, because of growing up with his grandmother. Julie had reminded him of Granny Morgan right from the start. Funny. People always looked at babies and said, "That one's got his mother's eyes," or his father's mouth, or Aunt Hattie's nose, and Will had always thought it was just a bunch of baloney. Until he looked at his baby girl that spring day eleven years ago. It wasn't the eyes, which were screwed tightly shut, or the mouth, which was wide open, or even the nose, which was hardly there at all.

It was something in the way he felt when he held the tiny bundle. A strength or power that he realized had been missing from his world since Granny Morgan died. Later, when Julie's eyes became a deep brown, he recognized the physical resemblance was there too. But it hadn't been that, not at first.

When the storm began it hadn't taken Will long to realize that this wasn't going to be just a light snow flurry. This was a full-fledged spring blizzard. The kind that closed the roads and knocked down power and telephone lines. Well, he was moving the last stack into the feed lot anyway. There was enough feed out and the cattle would be all right. He'd do chores early and call it a day.

He was in the house earlier than he expected. Charlie and Joe had beat him to the chores. He was grateful. The afternoon's work had tired him more than he cared to admit.

Now, in the warm kitchen, as he poured himself a cup of coffee, Will's only worry was whether Alice and the girls would get home before the roads got too bad. He didn't worry about her driving. Like all farm wives she could handle nearly any kind of vehicle on any kind of road. She'd done all the grain hauling before Charlie got his licence. Even drove the tractor. Tractors were the worst. He should know. Every year nearly fifty people injured in tractor accidents in Alberta—a dozen or more killed. If it weren't for Julie he'd have been one of those statistics. He remembered her face the first time he'd seen her after the accident. So pale and empty. She had done something, something more that just find him lying there under the tractor wheel, more than just digging under his chest so that he would have room to breathe. They had never talked about it but he knew it was not just shock that had kept her looking so weak and strained all winter. Something had sapped her strength and kept him alive.

Will stirred his coffee absentmindedly. Funny how he was thinking of Julie so much today. He wondered if they'd left town or decided to wait the storm out. Maybe he should phone the Co-op store and ask. Abbie Lenz would know. Paddy Behan claimed she "kept her finger on the pulse of the town." If they'd left they might have got as far as Behan's.

He peered out the window. Visibility was bad. He'd phone Paddy Behan and see. But first he'd put a bit of cream in his coffee, since Alice wasn't around to check up. He wished she'd never heard the word cholesterol.

Pouring the thick dollop, he remembered how he and Julie used to douse strawberries with it. Julie again. He shook his head. "The kid's really on my mind." He was just putting the cream back in the fridge when he noticed the note on the meat-loaf casserole. And then the power went out.

The response from the T.V. room, where howls from Jane and Billy proclaimed that they'd been cut off from some vitally important show, was enough to let Will know that it wasn't just a blown fuse. It took him a few minutes to put on his coat and check the power pole in the yard to make sure the outage covered a wider area than just their farm. Walking back to the house, he began to feel uneasy. Very uneasy. Before he phoned Behan's or Transalta Utilities he wanted to check something.

He had to take the meatloaf over to the window to read the note that was taped to it. "Mary," it said, "if I'm not home by three o'clock please put this in the oven." Why would Alice write that if Mary . . . and Julie were with her?

He was at the phone immediately dialing Behan's number. "Paddy! Are Alice and the girls at your place?"

"What girls?" Paddy laughed. "The only 'girls' here are my wife and yours! Just hold on, I'll let you talk to Alice."

It didn't take long for Will to realize the worst.

"No, of course they aren't with me!" Alice's voice became instantly shrill with alarm. "They'd gone to hunt for crocuses on the hill over by the old Tyler place, you know . . . they left around 11 o'clock, not long before I did . . . you mean they aren't back yet?"

"Now, Alice." Now that the crisis was clear, Will's voice became steady, dead calm. "They probably just went to the old buildings and are sitting out the storm there. Charlie and I'll take the skidoos and go get them." He paused, as Alice's panic seemed to radiate from the receiver in his hand. "You *stay* there, Alice. Now let me talk to Paddy."

After a few more protests from Alice, he could hear her voice in the background explaining to Mary Behan, then Paddy was on the line.

"Keep her there, Paddy, the roads are bad and it hasn't let up enough to see too far, and she's going to be too upset to drive. Power's out here but Jimmy can handle things. If we aren't back in an hour or two or if the storm lets up, see if you can make it. We'll take the old road allowance to the Tyler place, but we might have to search the fields between here and there if they got caught half-way. In three hours better get some more people organized . . . maybe the Mounties . . . but . . . don't say anything to Alice yet!"

"Right!" Paddy spoke louder than necessary. "You phone when you've got them home. We'll just wait here."

There was relief in Will's voice. "Thanks, Paddy." He hung up and found Charlie was waiting beside him.

Then he was giving orders and everyone was there moving like a team. Jane emptied the coffee pot into a thermos. Jimmy and Joe were putting together a box with parkas, boots, and scarves, while Charlie went to check to make sure the skidoos were gassed up. Billy dug out a couple of flashlights.

Outside, the storm didn't seem to have let up much and Charlie sat waiting for Will. Jimmy finished tying the box on one of the skidoos and Will climbed on.

"Jimmy," he said slowly, raising his voice to be heard above the wind, "if one of us isn't back in two hours, call Paddy Behan."

Jimmy nodded and ran back to the house.

The two skidoos edged into the storm. Bucking the wind, they would have had to go slowly anyway but the lack of visibility kept them in low.

Charlie steered for the fence line. Driving about two feet parallel to it was the only hope. But the terrain there was rough and would have made slow going at the best of times. They settled into the wind, Will watching for Charlie's brakelight through half-closed eyes, trying to remember each dip and bend of the road and always aware that the land was different, the slopes steeper. As long as they kept the fences in sight, they wouldn't miss the turn onto the old road allowance.

Chapter Twelve

Julie's head ached. It seemed to her that she had been staring at the house, warm and welcoming, moving toward it through the storm, the light from the kitchen window beckoning her. Was that Will sitting at the table looking out at her, moving across the room . . . ? And then suddenly the house was dark, still there, but no longer lit to guide her. She shuddered. And felt Mary's arm tighten around her.

"Did you drop off to sleep, Julie? I hope it's not hypothermia. Come on, maybe if you moved around a little." Mary got up and pulled Julie along. "Here, help me put some more wood on the fire."

The fire was burning well now that the old wood had caught and the dry boards added to it. Julie watched the smoke drift up to the roof of the old barn, remembering the phantom smoke she had seen on Christmas Day. She knew now it hadn't been just wisps of snow, and it had been over the north end of the barn, where the remains of the fire were.

Helping Mary pile more boards on warmed her a little. And now that Mary did not want her to see what was at the other end of the barn, she felt somehow protected, as if Mary were a buffer between Julie and the horror there.

"How are your feet, Julie? Mine are freezing!" Mary looked down at their soaked runners and socks.

Julie hadn't thought about her feet but she realized that they were ice cold too.

"Maybe we should take off our shoes and try to dry the socks and warm our feet at the fire . . . but first let's get some more of those boards." Mary pointed at a few planks in the southwest corner. "Come on! You can help me!"

As they passed the window both girls looked up hopefully, but it seemed as dark as ever and the snow swirled as if it would never slacken, never quit. Neither spoke.

Hauling the planks warmed them a little. They dropped their load near the fire.

"Maybe running on the spot would help warm us." Mary didn't sound too sure and Julie sat down, grateful to be in the circle of warmth thrown by the fire, still afraid to look at it. Always facing south, keeping her back to the dreaded north wall. She concentrated on trying to untie the wet knots that had formed in her shoelaces.

Mary looked at her watch. "Three o'clock. You didn't notice what time it was when we got here . . . ? No, of course not, you don't wear a watch, do you?" Mary gave her a little smile, ". . . and if you did you'd never look at it anyway." The smile faded. "I wonder how long we've been here . . . ?"

Julie had managed to get one shoe off and carefully hung her sock on a board jutting out of the fire. Walking around with Mary had taken away the numbness, and her foot began to tingle as she extended it to the fire. At least the pain gave her something to concentrate on, that and the hopelessly knotted lace on her other shoe.

"We left home at about eleven, so we would have got to the hill at around half past and then we spent about an hour, maybe more up there. . . . I knew we should have packed a lunch. . . . So maybe the rain started at one o'clock . . . the snow a bit later . . . the storm maybe one-thirty. . . . Did it take us half an hour to get in here? We've been here an hour anyway . . ."

Julie realized that Mary was talking less to express her thoughts than to break the silence, to keep going. She feels it too, she thought. Even if she's not aware of the oppression in here, she feels it. And I'm not being much help, not saying a word. But it was so hard, as if she had forgotten how.

"Dad's probably waiting for the storm to let up," Julie said, her voice strange to her own ears. She could feel Mary's relief and wished that she really believed it herself. The vision of Will in the dark farmhouse made her wonder.

She should try to go back, send her thoughts to the house, move through the storm, the way she had done before, but it was easier just to concentrate on her shoelace. Deep down she did not want to know that they were still not missed, that there was the chance they would be here when night fell. Still waiting.

It got dark around seven now, four more hours. And the storm could continue all night. The barn would be thick with evil, pressing in through the darkness. She couldn't bear to think about it, it made the screams echo in her head again.

"Yes, that's it. Dad knows we'd come here." Mary's voice held more confidence than she felt, Julie knew. They both knew that they might have been caught half way, be lost, wandering in the storm, huddled together somewhere in the snow by now. It happened.

"He'll just wait for the storm to let up a bit. No use looking for somebody when you can't see." Mary's voice almost broke.

She doesn't believe it, Julie thought. She won't quit but she's scared now. I've got to help her. Julie grasped the idea, almost with relief. She would put her mind to distracting Mary and distract herself as well. She stuck her foot out towards her sister. "Can you get this undone?"

Mary looked at her with relief. "First let's pull it off . . . you do tie 'em tight don't you." She tugged, almost falling in the fire when the shoe finally gave.

Julie pulled off her sock and looked at her foot, blue-white with cold. She held it toward the fire. This was really going to hurt.

And then she heard it. The familiar whine, just for a moment penetrating the howl and whistle of the wind around the eaves of the old barn.

"Listen!" she commanded.

Mary stopped struggling with the laces but all they could hear was the wind and, closer, the crackle of the fire as it bit into the age-softened wood.

Julie couldn't hear it again but she knew. And she smiled. "They're coming!" she said. "Dad and Charlie, on the skidoos . . . they're coming."

Mary looked at her. Puzzled. "I didn't hear anything. Are you sure, Julie?"

Julie nodded. "They're a long way off," she said, her voice sure now, "but they're coming." She grimaced, her foot beginning to tingle painfully.

There was relief in Mary's voice. "Well, if you think so . . . you've got the best instincts in the family." Mary had propped Julie's runner against one of the boards to warm. Now she knelt and grabbed the foot Julie had jerked away from the fire. "Don't warm it too fast, it'll hurt more that way . . . let me rub it a bit . . . that's better."

Mary was right, it was less painful. Still tingling but easier to bear. "What about your feet? They're just as wet. They must be just as cold?"

"I guess all the moving around helped." Mary sat back down beside Julie and began to take off her runners. "But you've got the right idea and dry socks would be nice . . . but not *that* dry!" Mary made a grab for the first sock Julie had hung at the fire and beat out the flames.

Julie held it up. The toe was still smoking and all that was left of it was a charred fringe. "It will be handy for wearing with thongs in the summer," she said ruefully.

Mary hugged her and laughed.

Julie felt relief welling up inside like a bubble about to burst. Why? She shouldn't feel happy, not here. But she did. And now there was no mistaking it. The whine of a motor, a skidoo, over the storm. This time Mary heard it too.

Chapter Thirteen

Julie never liked the skidoos. She hated the way they tracked up the smooth expanse of the winter fields, the way they allowed people to pursue animals through the winter bush. And she hated the shrill whine that cut through still winter days like an angry hornet magnified many times over. But at this moment it was the most welcome sound she had ever heard.

With the noise of the storm, it was hard to tell just where the sound was coming from but it was there all right. Close.

Mary was up and running to the south door, the one they had come through. Julie was struggling to get her sockless feet into her shoes when the door behind her burst open, the north door, and Will and Charlie were inside. Instantly, Mary was sprinting across the barn, past Julie, running towards Will, who stood with arms outstretched, waiting. Julie wanted to run to him too, but she couldn't. As much as she wanted to be with him the revulsion to the place he stood held her rooted to the spot. It was only when he and Mary came near that she was free to move. To find shelter.

"Sorry it took so long," Will said.

Mary was laughing and crying at once. "I . . . we knew you'd come here first . . . you did, didn't you? You didn't try to make it across the field, did you?"

Charlie had set down the box of clothes and was helping Julie into her down-filled parka. She had taken her cardigan off first. Even with the wet sweater underneath it felt warmer.

"We'll warm up a bit and then start back," Will said. "It's getting on to quarter to four." He poured some coffee into the thermos cup and handed it to Mary. Julie was next. She hated the bitter, coffee taste. Jane hadn't put any sugar in. But it was hot and that felt good. She made a face and drank again.

"We couldn't get in the house," Mary was saying. "You've got it too well boarded up. We almost missed the barn . . . you couldn't see anything in the storm . . . then Julie managed to get us here."

Julie knew Will's eyes were on her, but she didn't look up. She was busy pulling on the wool socks that were stuffed in her snowboots.

"Good thing we didn't board this place up. . . ." Charlie caught himself. The realization of what that might have meant stopped him. He stood, looking around the old barn, at the fire and the boards the girls had piled ready to burn. "You were prepared for a long stay?"

Mary didn't answer.

"We didn't know . . . we thought . . . you might wait for the storm to be over before you came." Julie couldn't express the fear that Will didn't know they were missing. ". . . We knew you'd come eventually."

"Dad . . ." Mary looked around. ". . . Somebody else has been here. . . ." She pointed to the north corner. ". . . There's been a fire over there . . . and . . . something else . . . I don't understand . . . you should look."

Charlie dug a flashlight out of his pocket and followed Mary and Will. Julie did not move. She hunkered down again close to the fire, carefully keeping her back to them and what they would see.

She heard Will's involuntary, "Damn!" and Charlie's, "So that's what happened to Behan's calf . . ." and she knew they were looking at the mutilated remains of the baby calf, the head separate and placed on a board. She also knew that they didn't see it as she did. Fresh blood dripping from the severed head, hands holding a basin to catch it. . . . And they didn't know what else there was, not far from where they stood.

"Why would anybody do that?" Mary's voice quivered a little.

"We'd better get going," Will said abruptly, bringing Mary back to the fire. "Julie'll ride with me and you and Mary follow."

Charlie came over and picked up the box. Mary handed Julie

54

a pair of mitts, pulled her own gloves out of her pocket, and began to follow Charlie to the door.

Julie's heart sank. They were going out the north door. She was sure she couldn't do it. Couldn't follow them—not that close. She looked wildly toward Will, who stood waiting for her. Somehow his calm helped. Maybe . . . if she walked on the other side of him, held his hand.

He reached down and helped her to her feet. "Ready?" he said. She pulled up her parka hood as if somehow she could hide inside. Walking as close as she could to him helped. A little.

They were almost to the door. For a moment Julie thought she would make it, then the screaming began. She could see the flames, darkness all around, hear rain on the old tin roof above, hear low voices, moaning, chanting, rising to a crescendo and still the screams predominated. Julie shut her eyes and crumpled against Will.

The next thing she knew was the snow licking at her face. It felt refreshing. Clean and sharp like the wind still whirling around. Will was carrying her.

"Do you want to go back in for a while?" he yelled.

"No!" She almost screamed the word. She could not have borne it. The barn loomed behind them, almost blotted out by the snow already.

Will helped her onto the skidoo and climbed on behind. The familiar whine of the motor vibrated into life. Even with the lights on they could see barely a skidoo length in front. The lights were probably no help at all, but the tail lights would guide Charlie and Mary if they stayed close behind.

Now Will was faced with steering through the maze of snow. The wind had picked up, and it was hard to tell if the whirling mass in front of them was falling or drifting snow. It had been easier coming in. Follow the fence line from the gate, open the gate above, and then keep steering with the downhill slope of the field until they came to the barn.

Another time they might have followed the tracks they made coming down, but even if they could have seen them, any signs had long since been obliterated by the drifting snow.

Will put Julie's mittened hands on the handlebars between

his own and bent to yell as close as the parka would allow. "Hold on and help me steer."

Julie knew he was really saying, "You have to steer across the field . . . you know where the gate is . . . help me." Only Will understood and trusted she could do it. She held on as the skidoo began to move.

Before long they had worked out a system. Will steered as straight as he could, trying to hold the skidoo so that it was always on an uphill slant. From time to time Julie would pull to left or right, holding him on track, heading in a direct line for the gate. She realized it was easy, like focusing your eyes on the end of a piece of cloth you were cutting, not looking at where you were but the spot where you wanted to end up.

They could have gone faster now, but Will held the speed down so that it would be easy for Charlie to keep their lights in sight. Frequently Julie could feel him turn, looking back to make sure the lights of the other skidoo were following.

Once out on the old road allowance, they could move faster, following the fence line and knowing that Charlie was not so dependent on them to guide the way.

Now Julie was feeling the cold, the chill creeping through her parka, her damp sweater feeling clammy and cold.

She was grateful at last when they pulled into the yard, following the caragana hedge the last bit of the way. She had looked forward to a welcoming brightness of the yard light, the shining windows, and was surprised that the house loomed in front of them, almost as dark as it had been when she had seen it last. Only a faint glow indicated light within.

Will rushed her inside and instantly she was surrounded by voices, the soft glow of the old kerosene lamp.

"Power's still off," Jimmy told Will. "I phoned. They said it'd be several hours."

"You'd better call Mum," added Joe. "She's been phoning every five minutes . . ."

". . . Ten . . . every ten minutes . . . don't exaggerate." Jane was helping Julie off with her things. "I bet you two'd like a hot bath . . . too bad . . . no power—no water pressure."

"Have you got enough water in the kettle to fill a couple

of hot water bottles?" Mary gestured to the kettle boiling on the gas stove.

Julie could hear Will on the phone, his voice reassuring, as she and Mary headed for the bedroom.

Curled up under the eiderdown, her toes curling around the edge of the hot water bottle, Julie began to warm up at last. Enough to drift into a comfortable sleep. As she dropped off she hoped there would be no dreams.

Chapter Fourteen

When Julie opened her eyes again the storm was over. Morning sunshine streamed through the bedroom window and her mother was standing next to the bed.

"Mum, you finally got home." Julie started to throw back the covers. "I guess I slept in, didn't I?"

"You can sleep in some more if you want to. It's still Easter break, you know."

By the time Julie came downstairs it was nearly ten o'clock. Mary was sitting at the kitchen table with her parents and Paddy Behan. The look on Alice Morgan's face was enough to tell Julie that they had been talking about the barn and what had been found there.

"We've phoned the R.C.M.P. detachment in Hurry and Sgt. Pearson's on his way. Going to come here and then we'll go show him the barn." Will looked straight at Julie. "Mary told me about the magazines. . . ."

"You didn't look at them, Julie?" Alice broke in. ". . . Mary, you said she didn't look at them! . . . that you tore them all up in *little* pieces?"

"Yes, Mum, I did." Mary looked at Julie and rolled her eyes.

"I didn't see them, Mum. Mary tore them up really fast . . . in *very* small pieces . . . and anyway I didn't look."

"She didn't," Mary insisted.

". . . And Charlie and I saw the calf . . ." Will continued patiently.

". . . And Julie never did . . . never even went near the thing!" Mary looked significantly at her mother.

"Think carefully, Julie," Will said looking straight at her. "Did you see anything else? Anything we should tell Dan Pearson when he gets here? Anything strange . . . or that hadn't been there other times when you were in the barn?"

"I never went in the barn . . ." Julie said slowly, " . . . ever before. . . . That was the first time."

Will looked the question at her.

"It made me feel . . . nervous . . . even before . . ." she finished. And looked straight at Will, hoping he would understand.

He nodded. And waited.

"But there was something . . ." She felt more confident now, turning to Mary for confirmation. "Those sticks you used for kindling . . ."

"That's right, Dad," Mary interrupted. "There were a couple of sticks loosely nailed to the wall. I pulled them down and used them, but I sort of thought it was funny . . . they were tied together . . . one was longer than the other. They're gone now. Burned."

Will was still looking at Julie expectantly.

". . . the way they were tied," she continued, ". . . was like a cross, but they were hanging upside down on the wall, just over the place where the fire had been . . ." she quickly corrected herself, ". . . where Mary said there'd been a fire."

Be careful, Julie thought, you almost said too much, you're not supposed to know about the fire, the calf's head. Watch it! She willed herself to sit very still, to hold her innocent expression, not to let on what she knew. She'd had a lifetime of practice.

She needn't have worried. Her last words had had an almost electric effect on her listeners. Alice said nothing but her quick intake of breath was all the more audible. Paddy Behan muttered, "Damn!" under his breath, and the look he and Will exchanged was solemn, almost angry.

Mary broke the silence, turning to Julie eagerly, "You're right, Julie! I never thought of it at the time, but you're right!" She looked at her younger sister admiringly. "You're a very observant kid."

Julie didn't have to say anything else. Everyone's attention

59

was focused by the sound of the car coming down the road and into the Morgan yard. Then Sgt. Pearson and a young Mountie who was introduced as Const. Jeffrey Kennedy were in the kitchen, and Julie moved back to stand by the door to the stairs, hoping to make herself inconspicuous.

Luckily, Mary was only too eager to describe everything. She even described the cross, as if she'd recognized it right away. Now and then Sgt. Pearson would ask her a question but she seemed to be directing her answers as much to the good looking young constable as to him.

"Better have you come along, Will. . . . Paddy, you've got to identify the calf," Sgt. Pearson got up. "Girls too, I suppose."

Julie's heart sank and she looked to Will for help. She couldn't go. Even in daylight, with everyone there, she did not want to face the barn again.

And then she sneezed. It was enough for Alice. "Mary can tell you everything you need to know about yesterday, Dan Pearson. I'm putting this girl to bed, before she comes down with a cold." She turned to Mary. "Are you sure you're feeling all right?"

"I'm just fine," Mary said, smiling brightly, and from the look young Const. Kennedy gave her it was obvious he thought so too.

Will was the last one to leave, and Julie was grateful that Alice was distracted with filling a hot water bottle and looking for the Vicks.

"Daddy," she said softly as she followed him to the door, "tell them to dig."

She turned and walked back to her mother, knowing that he had heard and would somehow get the message across.

She was in for an afternoon of treatment she didn't really need but it was worth it, the chest rubs, the vaporizer and all, just to avoid the barn. She sneezed again.

Chapter Fifteen

Mary sat in the back of the R.C.M.P. car with Paddy Behan while Will and Charlie rode the skidoos on ahead. Things were working out much better than she expected. She hadn't been looking forward to having to talk to the police. Not that she'd dreaded it exactly. It seemed she'd known Sgt. Pearson all her life, although she supposed he'd only been stationed in Hurry five or six years. But he was well liked in the district and a good friend of the family. She'd dreaded talking about the magazines, had almost not told anyone at all, but she realized they were important. Will had taken over and fielded that part of the questioning, suggesting that Mary write a statement, and Dan Pearson had agreed.

It was very exciting getting to ride in the "cop car," although she had to admit the fact that there were no door handles in the back bothered her at first. Once you were in, you were in, until somebody on the outside opened the door. And she would have preferred a different seating arrangement. Mr. Behan in the front and Jeffrey in the back with her. She supposed there was some regulation about it.

Still, this seating arrangement had its advantages. Sitting behind Sgt. Pearson this way, she had an excellent opportunity to notice what a nice profile his young constable had. She especially liked the way his hair curled behind his ear, in spite of the regulation haircut. She decided that his hair colour would be considered a dark blonde instead of light brown. It probably bleached out in the summer the way hers did. If only her mother would let her use a rinse on her hair, it wouldn't look so mousy now.

It was Sgt. Pearson who opened the door for her when they got to the corner by the old road allowance. They'd take the skidoos from there. The two Mounties began to unload theirs. Mary climbed up behind Charlie. No point standing around hoping that Jeffrey would offer her a ride. Will would have wondered what she was waiting for and said something, and anyway there was probably some regulation against that too.

When they arrived at the old barn Mary was disappointed again. It seemed that all she was needed for was to retrace her steps of the day before, where she had found the magazines, how they had been lying, where the cross had been nailed. The remains of the old fire was still obvious although there were just ashes now that she had taken away the unburned wood. Const. Kennedy began scooping the ashes into a plastic bag, and Paddy Behan and Sgt. Pearson were examining the calf when Will called Charlie to take her home.

"That's all they need you for now. You'll just be in the way." He led her to the door where Charlie was waiting. "I'd come too but I have something to talk to Dan Pearson about."

Mary looked back at Const. Kennedy. She felt as if she was being herded out. Knowing he was watching made it even worse. She sighed as she climbed on the skidoo behind Charlie. It had started out to be so . . . interesting this morning and now . . . She still had to go in with her statement, but she truly dreaded any questions she might be asked about the magazines. She'd die if Jeffrey Kennedy was there. It was turning out to be hopeless. Anyway, there was probably a regulation about an officer having anything to do with a witness in an investigation he was working on.

Will and Paddy came back to the Morgan house two hours later, tight-lipped and angry-looking. It took a few minutes to round up the whole family.

"What about Julie?" Mary asked.

"Leave her," Alice said, "she's sleeping."

But she wasn't. She had heard the men coming in and was huddled on the stairs, out of sight, listening as Will spoke.

"I don't want anybody going anywhere near that barn or

for that matter anywhere near the Tyler place for . . . until I say so. Got that?"

Joe and Jimmy exchanged glances. They had been planning to sneak over in the morning. It wasn't fair that Mary and Julie were the only eye-witnesses. They'd get a lot of mileage out of this at school.

Will caught the look and continued, "There are going to be R.C.M.P. from Red Deer and probably from K Division in Edmonton searching that barn for a while and *nobody*," he looked hard at Joe and Jimmy, "I mean *nobody* is going to go there."

There was a shocked silence. Not so much at the words as at the way Will spoke. Controlled anger and . . . something else.

It was Mary who finally broke the silence. "They found something else . . . after we left . . . didn't they?"

It seemed as if everyone had stopped breathing. Only Julie, crouched on the stairs, did not want to hear the next words.

Will sighed. "Yeah." He looked at the waiting, expectant faces.

Paddy Behan broke the silence. "They might as well know, Will . . . the news'll be all over Hurry district by tomorrow. Probably be on T.V. news." He waited for Will's nod before he continued. "There was a body . . . a young girl . . . teen-aged, I guess . . . nobody from around here. . . . They're checking missing kids. . . ." Paddy gave up trying to answer the barrage of questions pouring on him.

Will raised his voice over the racket as Jane headed for the telephone. ". . . And *nobody* is going to phone from here until Dan Pearson gets his report in! There'll be enough rumours about this by tomorrow, there won't be any starting from this house."

Julie crept back up the stairs to her bedroom. A girl, teen-aged . . . younger than Mary. . . . Not Joan of Arc tied to the stake . . . but another girl . . . another fire . . . a girl with long blonde hair . . . and screaming . . . awful screaming. She put her hands over her ears and fell on the bed. She really did feel sick now.

Paddy Behan was right. Except about the timing. By morning the Morgan phone was ringing off the hook. There had been a brief mention on the eleven o'clock news. By noon there was more. "An unidentified girl . . . blonde, long hair, no birthmarks, aged fourteen to sixteen." At six o'clock there was an artist's drawing of the girl's face. Police were still investigating. There was no mention of the cause of death. When Alice questioned Will, he just shook his head. "You don't want to know," he said grimly.

Julie stayed in bed. She was grateful that Mary's description of what they had done in the barn cleared her of the barrage of curiosity that was unleashed on Mary. Julie, according to Mary, had never moved from the fire. Never gone to the north end of the barn, had not seen the calf, the magazines, ". . . just sat there like a bump on a log."

On the third day, just when everyone was going back to school—something Julie had been dreading—she developed a fever. By that time the girl had been identified as a fifteen-year-old runaway from Vancouver. She was last seen in Edmonton the previous September.

"Imagine," said Alice on the phone to Mary Behan one morning, "just two years older than our Jane."

When news of the calf and the cross got out, it became a big story.

Will was disgusted. A T.V. news team had gone to the high school trying to get an interview with Mary as she boarded the bus. "What's going on with the world?" he complained to Paddy Behan. "A young girl's been killed by some maniac and everybody wants to know all the dirty details?"

"It's news, Will," Paddy reasoned. "Maybe some folks are after the sensationalism, but for most of 'em it's just a break from watching the news every night and seeing nothing but a bunch of politicians figuring out new ways to rip more taxes out of us."

The weather had warmed up, and the snow melted as quickly as it had come. Will's restriction on going to the old Tyler place didn't need any reinforcement, since the fields were far too muddy for crossing.

A camera crew got stuck trying to get down the old road allowance to the barn, and Will and Charlie spent two hours with logging chains and the tractor pulling their van out.

Will came back muddy and disgruntled. "The fools should've been able to see that wasn't a regular road. Couldn't get down it with a four wheel drive after that thaw. . . . If we hadn't had a winch we'd have got the tractor stuck!" He shook his head. "Wouldn't have done them much good if they had got there. The Mounties have got the place sealed off. They're going over it with a fine tooth comb."

"They'd probably be happy with just an outside shot of the barn," Jimmy said. "Maybe catch a shot of the detective and lab crew from Edmonton." Jimmy was interested in photography. It had started because he wanted to get shots of his horse Pinto and then he'd branched out and just photographed everything: horses, the family, the farm, old buildings. He hadn't told his father that the still photo of the Tyler barn the Red Deer T.V. station was using was one he had sold them.

It hadn't caused any concern when Inspector Pankhurst from Edmonton phoned that he would be coming out to question Will again. Julie watched from the upstairs window as he and Sgt. Pearson got out of the car. Sgt. Pearson looked worried, more worried than she'd ever seen him before. Maybe it was because he was nervous about having the Inspector with him, Julie thought.

Will met them in the yard and soon Julie could hear the voices in the kitchen. Her mother had gone to town for groceries, everybody else was at school, and her father would think she was asleep. Julie moved down and sat on the stairs where she could hear.

She soon realized why Dan Pearson didn't look too happy. An unfamiliar voice that must belong to the Inspector was questioning Will. A lot of questions. How long had he owned the barn? When last had he been there? The voice was slow, deliberate, then it changed.

"So Mr. Morgan, Sgt. Pearson tells me that it was your suggestion that they dig?"

There was no sound. Will must have nodded.

"Now just what would make you give that kind of advice . . . ?" The voice was hostile, insinuating.

"Oh Daddy," Julie wanted to cry, ". . . he thinks you . . . you had something to do with . . ." She could barely restrain herself from running into the kitchen.

"It seems unusual, Mr. Morgan? You had some kind of knowledge . . ."

Will's voice cut in, and though it would seem even and controlled to the Inspector, Julie was shocked by an edge of rage she had never heard in her father's voice before. He spoke slowly, as if explaining something to someone a bit dull-witted. "When I went to the barn with Sgt. Pearson, I noticed the dirt floor was uneven. I stored machinery in there for years. That floor was hard packed . . . should have been, anyway."

"Did that barn ever have a floor . . . a wooden floor, that is? There seems to be the remains of a floor in one corner."

"There was a tack room there . . . added on after the barn was built. Just a few years before Tyler moved off the land and I took over."

Slowly, the questioning took on a more normal tone and Julie let out her breath in a soft sigh of relief. Still, she knew the suspicion was there and she knew Will knew. And it was her fault.

Chapter Sixteen

Julie waited until the door closed and she heard the car start up and drive away before she went the rest of the way down the stairs and into the kitchen.

Will was sitting at the table. He straightened up when he saw her.

"Oh Daddy, I'm so sorry." She wanted to tell him to explain how he knew that they should dig. But what would he say? It's this way Inspector, I've got a daughter who senses things, you might say she has E.S.P., and she told me? She could just imagine the reaction to that. Anyway, she knew Will would never tell anyone about her. How could he explain her anyway, when she couldn't explain herself?

He held her and patted her shoulder, then held her at arm's length and gave her a rueful smile. "So you were listening? I might have known."

She was close to tears now. It was so unfair. Her father was so good, and to have him suspected because of her . . .

"Don't worry, Julie. I'm sure it won't go any farther. The police have to explore every possibility. I suppose I did seem to 'know too much'." Will shook his head. "You should have seen Dan Pearson's face, when he realized the line Pankhurst was taking. I thought he'd bust a blood vessel!" He gave a rueful laugh. "But we've got to look at the Inspector's side, I guess. . . . It must be pretty hard, trying to solve a murder where the victim comes from somewhere else and there's no connection. I guess random killings, if that's what this is, must be pretty frustrating."

Julie realized that Will's reasoned explanation was as much for his own benefit as for hers.

He looked at her, remembering something. "What I don't understand is the timing. That girl was killed sometime last year. But you said you'd never gone in there even as a little girl. Was it just dark and spooky, or was there something else?"

Julie thought a long time before she answered. "Something else, I'm sure of that," she said, "but I don't know what. I've tried to figure it out. The feeling was so much worse . . . so much stronger. . . . I felt it Christmas Day when we went skiing. . . . I don't remember feeling such . . . such . . . horror before. But there was something there when I was a kid too. Not the same. . . ." She shrugged hopelessly. "Maybe it's just me. Maybe I've changed."

"Well, I expect they'll dig up the whole place now, even old man Tyler's tack room. The Inspector's bound and determined to find out how many bodies I've got cached there."

Julie tried to smile with Will but they both knew that his attempt at a joke wasn't funny.

"The tack room," she asked, "was that the northeast corner?"

Will nodded.

"If there's anything to find, that's where it will be." Julie was uncertain. She was trying to remember the last time Billy and Jane had wanted her to play in the old barn. She'd been around seven then, and she'd almost stepped in the door, but it was the north door and she couldn't, because there was some old feeling, old hate. Something that had been overwhelmed by the more recent death when she was there the other day.

The next day there were reports of another murdered girl, a hitchhiker found in an abandoned barn west of Calgary, and the Hurry story became old news. Inspector Pankhurst left hurriedly to consult with the officer covering that killing, fuelling speculation by the news media that there were similarities.

The digging in the Tyler barn continued under Sgt. Pearson's supervision.

Dan Pearson dropped by the Morgans for coffee as soon as he could and made a point of asking casually, "What was the date you had that tractor accident last September, Will? The 15th?

I thought so. Thought you might like to know, we've got somebody who says they saw that girl in Edmonton on the 17th." Sgt. Pearson stirred his coffee thoughtfully. "You were in hospital for quite a time, weren't you . . . a month, six weeks? Laid up pretty well all fall?"

They discussed the fall crops, the weather and when the sergeant left Alice shook her head. "Dan Pearson must really be under a lot of strain from this case. He made no sense at all, talking about the case one minute, your accident the next, then the crops, the weather . . ."

Will smiled. "Dan's all right. He's got a job to do but he's a damn good friend."

Julie went back to school the next day, grateful that Jane and the boys had fielded all the questions about the discovery on the Morgan property, only to find that she had another problem.

Susan Brown hunted her down during morning recess as if she were some long lost friend. "Julie, you were right!"

Julie stood there, puzzled by the outburst.

"You said I'd go to Edmonton for Easter holidays and I did!" Susan's exuberance had attracted several of the other students, and of course there were the popular girls who always hung around with Susan. Everybody gathered round as Susan explained, "Julie and I were playing E.S.P., and she said I was going to go, and I didn't see how that could possibly be because we don't have any relatives there and we don't go to visit, but . . . Mum's cousin from Calgary moved there and she and I went up to help her unpack and get settled. So I went, just like Julie said I would! You're good, Julie. How about telling me what else is going to happen to me!"

And then there were questions from all over. "And me, Julie . . . ," "Tell me . . . ," "Will I pass the Math test?" and then someone said, "Do you read palms?" And suddenly there were all these hands poking in Julie's face as everyone crowded around.

"It was just a silly guess," Julie protested. She remembered she'd been trying *not* to read Susan's mind. "It was an accident . . . a fluke or something." Julie's heart sank. Looking at all the eager faces, she remembered how she used to yearn to be popular, one of the "in crowd." What was it Miss Johnson had said once about being careful what you wish or it might come true in a way that wasn't nice at all? Now she was the centre of attention and she just wished they'd all go away.

When the bell rang and they went to line up, she found to her dismay that the girls were actually arguing over who would stand next to her. It didn't help either that during the next period Miss Friesen brought up the topic of careers. Everyone was to write about what they wanted to be. In the usual discussion before they started, Sonja Pawluk volunteered the information that "Julie's probably going to be a fortune teller." Of course everybody laughed.

Worse still, there was still the noon hour and last recess to get through. Julie felt dismal.

To her everlasting relief, by noon the school was abuzz with something far more interesting than Julie's inadvertent prophecy to Susan Brown.

Chapter Seventeen

The R.C.M.P. had uncovered human bones buried in the old Tyler barn. For once, the kids had the news first. Simon Dueck had been home with the flu and overheard his mother talking to Abbie Lenz. Duecks were one of the first families to have an extension phone, so Simon was able to eavesdrop on both sides of the conversation and get all the details. And with Abbie Lenz, that was probably as much as Inspector Pankhurst himself knew at this point.

Two skeletons had been discovered buried, in a different corner of the barn than the girl's body. Deeper, carefully dug graves. It looked like a bullet hole in one of the skulls. Abbie got that tidbit of information from her cousin's husband's sister whose boyfriend from Edmonton had been helping with the excavation.

Of course, one place the Hurry folk were way ahead of the police was in local history. These were old bones. Probably dated back to when the farm still belonged to the Tylers. None of the kids remembered old man Tyler. He'd sold out and gone into the nursing home in Hurry twenty years before. Wasn't there a Tyler buried in the Hurry cemetery?

Speculation raced around the school yard. After Simon, the Morgan kids were the main focus of questions. After all their dad owned the land and they'd played in the barn and house.

Hadn't Tyler always lived alone, an old bachelor farmer? "No," Billy remembered. "Dad was talking to Mum once about how sad it was that Tyler's son didn't even show up for the old man's funeral, but that maybe he didn't know, and nobody knew where he was or how to contact him."

"Yeah, Dad felt sorry for old Tyler because his son left home and never wrote or anything," added Joe. "I think Dad said he joined the army as soon as he was old enough to enlist, fought in World War II or Korea or something."

"So what happened to Mrs. Tyler? There must have been a Mrs. Tyler." Susan Brown and her friends had completely lost interest in Julie.

"Don't know . . . never heard anything about her."

"There weren't any ladies' things in the house, and no remains of curtains or anything like that . . . when we used to play there," Jane contributed.

Julie turned away. That wasn't exactly true. What about the teapot? The tiny doll's teapot she'd found that long ago summer? Sort of an orangey colour it was, with tiny flowers—she still had it tucked away at home in the box with her old dolls. She moved carefully to the edge of the group. Jane was busy describing the house, the water-stained patch of wall paper in what had been the parlour, the old cast iron kitchen stove. Had there been a little girl too? If so she'd never heard of one. She must remember to look for the teapot when she got home.

In the staff room Mr. Gordon was the centre of attention. He'd retired from teaching the previous spring, but came in occasionally to substitute. He wasn't popular, too apt to tear a strip off some new teacher who made small talk. "Gilbert Gordon doesn't suffer fools gladly," local folks said. Usually the other teachers gave him a wide berth but today they were glad to have him in school. If Abbie Lenz knew everything that went on in the Hurry district these days, Mr. Gordon knew everything that had happened there within the last fifty years. If anybody could cast some light on who was buried in the old Tyler barn it would be him.

He didn't fail them. Mr. Gordon had a theory all right. He probably could have told it in twenty-five words or less too, but he wasn't about to. He would begin at the beginning and go on to the end, with a fair bit of embroidery in the middle. He rather got a kick out of having all these young smart aleck teachers, with their theories and psychology and lesson plans coming out their ears, hanging on his every word. The only member of the entire teaching staff who didn't was Miss Johnson, who had picked up her cucumber sandwich and left for the library when he began.

Still, he had managed to drag on the history of how Zachariah Tyler had come to homestead in the Hurry district in 1908 . . . or was it 1907? No that was the year his uncle Ranfurley had arrived . . . of course he'd moved on in 1910, or was it 1911?

Mr. Gordon was certainly a gold mine of Hurry history. He was able to supply details nobody particularly cared to hear, like the big hailstorm of 1917, the hopper infestation in '21 (or was it '20?). His audience fidgeted, but they listened. And now and then they were rewarded.

"Zach Tyler married a girl from up north, somewhere around Vegreville or Vermilion. Magda something-or-other. Pretty girl, good worker too. I remember my dad saying there was a bumper crop that year. Prices were good too. Bumper crop next year." Mr. Gordon glanced at the clock. Two more minutes and the buzzer would go. He smiled; he was timing this just right. ". . . And the year after that. So much grain to be hauled that Zach Tyler got a hired man from somewhere up north . . . his wife's neck of the woods." He paused and looked at the clock expectantly. There wasn't a sound in the staff room.

"Fellow stayed on. Young Nicodemus was born in '28 . . . no, could've been '29. It was about four years later," he paused dramatically, ". . . the district was rocked by scandal. . . ." The silence of the staff room was shaken by the buzzer and Gordon finished triumphantly, "Magda Tyler and that hired man had run off . . . just disappeared together." Not one teacher moved. Mr. Gordon shook his head and began to gather up some papers he'd brought in to mark. "They said old Zach Tyler went a little crazy when that happened. He claimed he was going to start training riding horses of all things, built himself a fancy tack room in the barn, but nothing came of it. . . ." He paused at the door, pleased with himself. "I expect that's where they found the bodies . . . under that old tack room floor."

If he'd ever wanted undivided attention he had it now. All eyes were riveted on him, not one person had moved. He scowled triumphantly at them. "Isn't it time you teachers got back to work? This is a school, you know!"

Mr. Gordon was on outdoor supervision the last recess, and he got the same undivided attention he'd had in the staff room. Many of the students knew as much about him as he did about them. He'd taught their parents, in some cases their grandparents, and there was mutual respect. Questions flew thick and fast and this time Gil Gordon's answers were short and to the point.

"No, Billy, I don't remember Magda Tyler. 'Course everybody felt sorry for Zach Tyler when she left him."

"No, I don't think there was any mention of somebody *seeing* her leave with the hired man. Just that one day they were both gone. Folks assumed and I don't suppose Zach Tyler corrected their assumptions."

"Young Nick? I'd say he was about four or five when his mother left . . . disappeared."

"No, there was just the one child. No little girl . . . why do you ask, Juliet?"

Julie shrugged and tried to blend back into the crowd around Mr. Gordon. He was looking at her, as he often did, with a blend of curiosity and concern. Everyone else had been asking questions, getting answers with no questions asked in return and she'd thought she could too. But Mr. Gordon had always treated her differently. He'd told her once that she was the seventh child of a seventh child and so he expected great things of her. His dad had known Granny Morgan, he said another time. Julie was glad she'd never had him for a teacher, because the expectations would have been hard to face day after day. She was grateful when Simon Dueck asked a question, but even then Mr. Gordon continued to look at her, and Simon had to ask again before he got the old teacher's attention.

Chapter Eighteen

The Morgan supper table that night was so noisy with questions that Alice finally declared a Complete and Utter Silence time. Joey called it CUSS time, the extra S, he said, stood for "Stupid."

Billy and Jimmy were clearing the table in disgusted silence when Paddy Behan's truck pulled up. They exchanged smiles. Paddy would have some news: a couple of the lab men from Edmonton were staying at Behan's. If Will knew anything he wasn't telling them he'd surely tell Paddy.

Mary and Alice served pie and coffee. And Paddy began, "Have you folks heard the latest?" He didn't wait for a reply, "Both shot. One in the head, close range and one in the back. Amazing how they can tell something like that after all these years."

"To think that folks just accepted that they'd run off," Alice shook her head. "And felt sorry for the awful man!"

"Now Alice," Will said, "you've got the man tried, convicted, and off to the gallows."

"So has everybody in Hurry, Will. . . . Thanks, Alice, I will have some more of that coffee. . . . You've got to admit that business about the tack room and training horses was a mite strange. The man didn't have a decent piece of horseflesh on the place. I'm with Alice on this one. Everything points to Old Zach. 'Course it's not apt to come to anything and the police haven't even identified the bodies yet!"

"You have to admit, Will, Zach Tyler was a hard man to deal with."

"That's true Alice, but there used to be a lot of the old-timers didn't have much truck with socializing. That's why some of them came out West to begin with. No crime in that."

"Hell," added Paddy, "even Zach's own sister wouldn't have anything to do with him."

Joe forgot himself and butted in, "Mr. Tyler had a sister?"

"Yeah . . . she came out from England after the first war and taught school a while. Married a farmer near Bashaw. Came to visit Zach once or twice and then wouldn't have anything to do with him. Don't remember her name. . . ." Paddy exchanged a look with Will and cleared his throat. "I've been meaning to ask you to take a look at that seeder of mine . . . maybe you could drop around tomorrow."

It didn't take the kitchen long to clear after Paddy Behan left. Julie and Jimmy were just finishing the dishes when Jane came in.

"Where's that miniature cast iron stove that used to be on the window sill? Mum said I could take it to school. Johnson's reading *The Borrowers* to the Grade threes and us library helpers get to make a display of all kinds of miniatures and doll stuff."

Julie left Jane to hunt and slipped up to her room. She'd almost forgotten the teapot. She found it in the bottom of the box of dolls, just as she thought. For a long time she stared at the shiny orange and blue china. Sometimes she could know about the person who'd owned something if she held it like this. She was curious about the little girl who'd left this in the Tyler house. But tonight all she could think of was Miss Johnson arranging things for *The Borrowers* display. She carefully wrapped the teapot in tissue and put it in her lunch kit.

When she got to the library the next afternoon, the display had already been set up. She was holding the unwrapped teapot in her hand, when Miss Johnson turned and saw it.

"Julie! How did you get that?"

The question didn't seem to make sense. And then Julie saw the set of tiny orange dishes on the shelf behind Miss Johnson. There were several cups and saucers, a few larger plates, and even a cream and sugar—but no teapot. The teapot that matched was obviously the one Julie held in her hands.

"I . . . I found it. . . ."

Before she could answer, Miss Johnson had taken it and held it up, her face bright with remembering. "It's lustre ware . . . it was my mother's from when she was a little girl, but I . . . it disappeared. . . ." Miss Johnson's face clouded, and then she looked sharply at Julie.

Surely she couldn't think Julie had stolen it? No, that was not it. But someone had, and Miss Johnson knew.

"I found it," said Julie, ". . . in the old Tyler house . . . a long time ago. But how?"

"That awful boy . . . Nicodemus . . . my cousin . . . took it."

Julie felt a jolt of surprise. That explained why she had thought of Miss Johnson last night. But why had nobody mentioned that there was still a relative of the Tylers in the Hurry district? ". . . I . . . I didn't know. . . ."

"Very few people do," said Miss Johnson curtly, "and those who do are decent enough to keep quiet about it. There were . . . incidents . . ."

It was as if a mask had dropped over the librarian's face, and Julie did not so much see as sense the pain, the old anguish, and beneath it all, fear. Sharp and fierce, the way only a child can feel fear.

"My mother wouldn't have anything to do with old Zach. She tried to help him once after Aunt Magda left but then . . ." Again Julie could feel the pain and fear but now they were over-ridden and when Miss Johnson spoke again her voice was tight with anger.

"I just thank God she never knew. . . ."

Miss Johnson placed the teapot on the shelf and arranged the other tiny dishes around it. "Thank you for bringing this. . . . When we've finished with the display, I'd like you to have the whole set. You seem to be the kind of person who treasures and cares for things."

Julie beamed at her. "Thank you. I'll take good care of them."

Does everyone have a secret? Julie wondered as she left the library. Things were kept hidden for different reasons but mostly because . . . because they were really nobody else's business. She remembered Jane talking about how puzzled she'd been the first time she heard someone saying, "Oh they've got a skeleton in their closet," about one of the Hurry families. "I could hardly wait to get over to their place and check all the closets! Then Mum explained what it meant and said everyone's got at least one. I don't think I really understood for a long time. . . . For years afterwards every time I opened a closet I sort of expected to see a skeleton!"

Everybody's got a secret. . . . Miss Johnson and I do anyway. Some even have skeletons. But old Zach Tyler's were real.

Chapter Nineteen

There were no new developments in the investigations. Although the official word was that Magda Tyler and Orest Franchuk had been killed by "person or persons unknown," the case was closed as far as folks in the Hurry district were concerned. The building of the tack room was all the evidence they needed.

The other murder remained unsolved but it had a very definite effect. Parents were demanding that their daughters be accounted for at all times. No walking home alone, no staying by themselves. Everybody was careful. And Abbie Lenz was keeping a list of the licence numbers of all the strange vehicles that came into town. It was amazing she got any work done at all.

Of course, there weren't that many strangers who came to Hurry. A few people passing through on the highway who stopped for gas or a meal, occasional visitors, and sometimes a salesman or a businessman.

It was several weeks later when Julie saw the man. She was sitting on the ledge along the front of the Co-op store in Hurry waiting for her mother to come out. She'd been there for some time, her knees hunched up with her arms around them, watching ants going into a hole in a crack in the sidewalk. Seeing their living quarters down below. Staring hard. Uncomfortable the way she always was when she saw things she knew no one else could. Guilty somehow. She didn't even realize he was there until the shadow fell across her. Then she looked up and saw him. And she shivered in spite of the warmth of the day and the bright spring sunshine.

For a moment, a moment only, she looked in his eyes. They were old eyes and they made her feel old. Hundreds of years old. As if she were Joan of Arc. And she knew that eyes like that had watched Joan as the flames rose around her. Eyes like that had watched others burn throughout history. Old eyes, cruel eyes, without pity or remorse. And she stood up, turned, and fled into the store. But when she turned and looked out the window the man was gone, as if he had never been there, as if she had imagined it all. And though she went over to the counter where Abbie Lenz was packing the last of Alice's groceries, she never said a word about the man.

The following week when she went to town with Will and Jane and Billy, there was another stranger coming out of the store. Young this time, smiling and friendly. He was even willing to talk to Billy about the big Harley Davidson parked just down the street. He was open-faced and probably in his late teens with his long hair pulled back in a pony-tail.

"So, how much are you going to give me to buy the bike?" he joked to Billy.

Julie could see the awe in Billy's eyes as he stared at the shiny, black machine. Even Jane hung around, laughing at the young man's jokes.

Julie wished she could see his eyes, but he was wearing those reflecting sunglasses, so all she could see was herself and Jane and Billy. She realized she was backing away, not knowing why she felt uneasy, yet stifling the impulse to turn and run. They were perfectly safe, here in the sunshine, in the middle of the street where everybody could see. Still, she turned and hurried into the store, looking for her father.

Will wasn't there. Abbie Lenz said he'd gone to the lumber yard and she went back outside. Billy was sitting on the motor-cycle now, and the sight of it brought Julie running.

"Billy!" She realized she wasn't sure what to say but she had to get him away. ". . . Dad wants you . . . over at the lumber yard . . . says you should hurry." Her mouth felt dry.

Billy reluctantly climbed down and headed for the lumber yard. Julie would have followed, tried to explain, or somehow signalled to Will so that her lie would not be discovered, but now, she realized, the stranger's attention was focused on Jane. Or was it? She sensed hostility in her direction: go away little girl was the message. She stared back at the mirror-like glasses defiantly. "Come on, Jane, Abbie Lenz just about has Mum's groceries packed. We could start carrying them to the car."

Jane turned away from the motorcycle and started to follow her when Billy rushed up and grabbed Julie by the arm. "You just sent me on a wild goose chase, Julie. Dad didn't want me at all!" He gave her a shake. "But he does want *you* to go and phone Mum and see if she wants anything else before we leave town. *And that's not a lie!*"

He let go and Julie stood a moment rubbing her arm before turning and walking into the store. Behind her she could hear the stranger's laughter.

She had to go into the office at the back of the store to make her phone-call because Abbie Lenz was on the phone out front. It meant she couldn't watch the street. She was still on the phone when she heard the motorcycle roar to life a few minutes later. Her first impulse was to run out, but her mother was reminding her to check and see what fresh vegetables there were and not to get any lettuce if it looked wilted.

When Julie finally came out of the Co-op store she could see Jane by the car talking to Will, but Billy was nowhere in sight. Her feeling of misgiving grew, and she realized her heart was pounding. Even before she heard what Jane was saying to Will, she knew something was terribly wrong.

". . . So this guy's going to give Billy a ride to the farm on his motorcycle . . ."

"No!" Julie did not realize she had spoken aloud, screamed the word, until she saw their startled faces turned towards her. She started to run down the street, then stopped, knowing it was hopeless.

"Oh grow up, Julie. You are *such* a chicken! Why shouldn't Billy get a ride on that machine?" Jane was angry. "I'd have gone myself . . . in fact the guy wanted to take me . . . except everybody's so paranoid around here about girls doing anything since that body was found, I knew Mum and Dad would kill me!"

"It's not just girls. . . ." Julie said softly, staring down the road.

Will had been looking at her, puzzled, then he moved. "Get in. We'll just head along home right now." He had his hand on Julie's shoulder, guiding her to the front seat. "You ride in the back, Jane."

"Just a rangy-tanged minute," Jane protested, "it's my turn to ride in the front, Julie rode . . ."

Will gave her a look. "Get in the back this time," he said quietly.

Jane opened the door, settled in as the car started to move. "This is ridiculous. What's it going to be? . . . A twenty minute ride, tops."

"How long ago did they leave?" Will interrupted.

"Just a couple of minutes before you came out of the store . . . I don't know why you're both . . ."

". . . And they headed this way out of town . . . ?"

"Of course . . . ," Jane said in disgust, ". . . they were headed for the farm. How else would they go?" Jane leaned back and placed her feet deliberately on the back of Julie's seat, pushing as hard as she could. "Honestly Dad, just because Julie's being a fusspot!"

Julie said nothing. She had never been so frightened. Not in the barn at Easter, not ever before in her life. It surprised her to realize how physical the feeling was. A pressure building in her chest, it seemed she couldn't breathe fast enough. When had this started? Just since they'd left town. Before she'd been worried, had a sense of foreboding, but this had hit suddenly.

They had driven a couple of miles, just across the intersection of the grid road that would cut over to the highway, when her arm began to hurt, then her cheek stung as if she had been slapped—hard. She started to raise her hand to her face but somehow couldn't seem to lift it.

She was hardly aware that Will had increased speed until the car seemed to eat up the remaining miles. There was the farmyard ahead.

Jane's voice broke the silence. Gone was the confident, taunting tone, ". . . no motorcycle in the yard . . . maybe he just dropped him off and left . . ." There was doubt in Jane's voice now.

Will stopped the car abruptly, slammed it into park, and yanked on the emergency brake. Then he was out of the car, moving in long strides toward the house with Jane running behind.

Julie did not, could not, move. Her wrists hurt. She felt shaken, then pain seemed to come so fast—her side, her back, her head hurt. She felt woozy now, making it hard to think. But through it all she knew that Billy had not come home.

And then Charlie and Alice were out of the house, running to the truck with Jane close behind. Will had opened the car door and was just getting in, calling back to Mary, who stood in the doorway.

"If Sgt. Pearson calls back, tell him Alice is on her way to make a report, and I've gone to try to figure out which way they went from town." Will had backed the car around before he noticed Julie slumped white-faced on the seat beside him.

He reached over to touch her, and it was only when she cringed away that he realized that she was not aware of his presence at all. He took a deep breath and began to speak in a calm, careful voice.

"Julie . . . Julie . . . can you hear me?"

Julie turned her head slightly toward him.

"Julie . . . do you know who I am? You've got to listen to me . . . try to answer me." He had pulled the car over to let Charlie pass in the truck as soon as he reached the main road.

"Daddy . . ." Julie answered softly.

He stopped the car and turned to her. "That's right. Now listen to what I'm going to say. Concentrate on me and what I'm saying. Then maybe you can tell me what you're feeling." Will looked at her steadily. ". . . And maybe it will help us to figure out what we should do." He put the car in gear and began to drive slowly down the road toward town.

"When your great-granny Morgan first came to Canada as a young woman," he began slowly, "her youngest brother was working in the coal mines back in Wales . . . and one day there was an accident, a cave-in or something. Anyway, she was over here in Canada, but she knew something was wrong. And she had a terrible pain in her right arm. She couldn't use it at all, and nobody could figure out what was wrong with it. Then they got word about her brother being missing."

"They didn't find him until he was dead."

Will hardly recognized Julie's voice, it was flat, lifeless. "I wasn't going to tell you that part," he said ruefully, "but you're right." Will began again. "What I was going to tell you was that when they found him, rocks had fallen on his right arm and crushed it . . . and somehow she'd known."

Julie nodded. "Yes," she said, "that's how it is. My arm hurts, and then my face and my wrists and my side and back." Her voice rose steadily, ". . . and then . . . oh everything! I can't think anymore, it's just black . . ." She began to sob.

Will's voice was calm, pulling her back, steadying her.

"All right Julie, don't think about Billy anymore . . . try to think about the motorcycle. You saw it in town. . . ."

Julie nodded.

"Just think about it."

They were nearing the intersection two miles from town. Julie shut her eyes. "It wasn't here . . . I'm sure it wasn't here." Her voice became excited as they entered the intersection. "It turned here!" She pointed and heard Will's sharp intake of breath before she opened her eyes.

She was pointing down the road to the highway. Will swung the car around to turn, his face grim.

Chapter Twenty

As they drove slowly down the grid road, the fear returned, sweeping over Julie, fresh and terrible. But now she understood. It had been only after the motorcycle turned, not going the way it was supposed to, that Billy began to be afraid. She tried to concentrate on the motorcycle, but before they had reached the next road allowance, she knew something was wrong. The hurt was starting again, sharp and clear, the way it had before. The burning cheek, the pressure on her wrists, the other pain and the clouding over of her mind no matter how she fought it. And she could no longer visualize the motorcycle on the road.

"Daddy," she murmured, "I can't . . ." and slumped over in the seat.

Will had been watching her with growing concern and now he pulled the car over. He reached over to Julie. She was breathing all right, but pale and crumpled as if she had fainted. He'd better get her home as soon as possible. The road was too narrow for a U-turn just here, so he'd have to back a little. No, there was the entrance to Jim McDermid's hayfield along here. He could back into that.

He was almost past it, pulling by so that he could back in, checking it to make sure backing would be safe, when he saw the tracks. Not ruts—the ground was dry and hard—but pressure marks, as if a vehicle had been there not too long before. He wanted to get out and investigate, but one look at Julie changed his mind. She was gasping for breath, paler than she'd been before. He had to get her away from this spot. He drove quickly to the intersection just ahead, checked for traffic, made a U-turn,

85

and sped back along the road they had come. As he neared the intersection, Julie's breathing became normal again. By the time they were within a mile of home, she opened her eyes and sat up.

"I'm sorry . . . I guess I wasn't much help." Julie was close to tears. "I don't know what's wrong . . . I *want* to think about Billy . . . try to feel what's happening, but . . . I can't. It's almost like my mind jerks back . . . like your hand does if you try to put it in a fire." She thought of Joan then, flames around her. She wanted so much to be normal, to be without these terrible thoughts and feelings.

Will reached over and patted her hand. "Never mind, maybe it wasn't such a good idea. . . ." he said gently. "But maybe we learned something."

Mary was out the door and running to the car before it had stopped in the yard.

At first Julie thought she was going to tell them something, then she realized that Mary was looking in the back of the car hopefully as if expecting Billy to be there.

"You came back so soon . . . ," she said as they climbed out of the car, "I thought . . . "

"I think your sister needs to lie down for a while," Will said, helping Julie out of the car.

Mary looked puzzled. "What's wrong?"

Will eyed his eldest daughter speculatively, as if wondering what he could tell her, what she would understand.

The phone was ringing as they entered the kitchen. Will was beside it in two strides but Mary beat him to it.

"Yes, Const. Kennedy . . . ?" she said eagerly. "No . . . no . . . he hasn't come home," her voice seemed to fail her, and she handed the phone to Will who listened a few minutes and then hung up.

"Pearson's on his way back from Red Deer, coming straight here. Your mother's on her way home too." He spoke to Mary. "Let's get your sister to bed, she's not well."

Julie was grateful to lie down. She was feeling nauseous now. She shut her eyes and the room seemed to spin, as if the bed was turning with her on it. It seemed to be better with her eyes open. She tried to focus on Mary's face. No, it was Jane's, then her mother's. When had they got home? She heard men's voices, cars coming and going in the yard. Everything swirled around her and she was just lying here. Helpless. Useless. Finally, she slept.

Alice Morgan watched Will drive out of the yard in Dan Pearson's police car. She had carried the coffee cups to the sink. She should wipe the table, maybe have a coffee herself. The phone kept ringing, not always the Morgan number, as people in the Hurry district spread the news. She wished they'd stay off the line in case somebody had some news for them . . . in case Billy got a chance to phone . . . from wherever he was.

Mary was standing by the window. As if watching would make a motorcycle come in the yard, bringing Billy home.

"That's the fourth time you've wiped the table, Mum." Jane looked up from the list she and Joe had compiled. Names and phone numbers of Billy's friends, places he might have gone instead of coming home. They'd phoned every likely person, and now they were starting on the unlikely ones.

The phone rang. Their number. Jimmy got it first. He listened a minute, thanked the caller, and hung up.

"Pete Mazurski says he saw that motorcycle driving by his place on the Hurry road around 2 o'clock."

"That was *before* . . . if he'd seen it later it might have been of some use!"

"Now Joe . . ." Alice was wiping the counters now, ". . . he's just trying to be helpful. Every bit of information helps."

Mary nodded. "I'll make a note of that . . . we should tell Jeff . . . Const. Kennedy." She sat down and took some of Jane's paper. "I'm going to write down everything we know . . . the times and everything. What time did you first see the guy on the motorcycle, Jane?"

"Oh for Pete's sake, Mary!" Joe threw down his pencil in disgust. "Who do you think you are? Nancy Drew, girl detective?"

Mary didn't say anything at first. "It's something to do," she said softly, blinking away tears.

Joe looked chastened. "Aw . . . I'm sorry, Sis . . . I didn't mean . . ."

The evening dragged on. Mary Behan came over with a roast,

and she and Alice made sandwiches. Charlie and Paddy had driven from farm to farm. It seemed that the only sighting of Billy on the motorcycle had been at Benoit's garage, just as they were leaving town. Remi Benoit had looked up from a car he was fixing, and Billy had waved to him. He'd noticed Will drive by too, about five minutes later.

There was more information when Sgt. Pearson dropped Will off. There were unmistakable signs of a vehicle having parked by the road near McDermid's hayfield, signs of activity, rosebushes trampled, but the ground was too hard for footprints although there were traces of maroon paint on a sapling near the fence line. Dan Pearson had cordoned off the area and radioed for the lab people.

"He's sticking his neck out, moving this fast. Normally they have to wait on a missing kid report. But he knows us . . . knows Billy's not a runaway."

"Oh, Will," Alice sobbed, "how could Billy do something so stupid?" She blew her nose hard. "If he were to walk in that door this minute, I wouldn't know whether to hug him or slug him!"

Will held her close. "You'd hug him, Alice, you know you would."

The phone rang then. Const. Kennedy calling. "Thought you might like to know, Mr. Morgan. Mr. McDermid noticed a maroon van parked by his hayfield when he went to town just after lunch. Nobody in it. He noticed the licence plate, but it was pretty dirty, couldn't tell the number, just that it was an Alberta plate."

Alice poured Will another cup of coffee. It was going to be a long night.

Chapter Twenty-one

Julie was dreaming. She was floating near a ceiling somewhere. Looking down. It was too dark to see anything. She could hear though. Laboured breathing and another sound. Wind in the trees? No, she remembered it from a camping trip, the sound of river water lapping against the bank. If only it wasn't so dark. She couldn't see who was lying there but she knew who it was. She called.

"Billy . . . " softly at first, then louder and louder. She had to wake him, but he didn't move. She was trying to scream, but her voice wasn't working. "Billy! Billy!"

Then she was being shaken. Her father's voice: "Wake up, Julie!" and she opened her eyes to see Will's anxious face above her.

"You were screaming," he said, brushing the hair away from her forehead. "You were dreaming about Billy." It was not a question.

Julie nodded.

Will was staring at her, despair in his eyes. "Was he . . . ?"

Julie reached for his hand. He knew she'd know and it was a relief not to have to pretend, to cover up. "He's alive," she said firmly.

Will let out his breath and sat down on the bed beside her. "Tell me the dream."

"There's not much to say. It was dark, too dark to see, except that it was inside somewhere. I . . . I couldn't see anything but I could hear. Someone breathing. I knew it was Billy . . . I was trying to call him . . . to wake him up . . . but I couldn't make a sound." Julie smiled sadly, "I guess I was making sounds all right, if you're here!"

Will smiled at her and nodded. "Was there anything else? Anything at all that you remember?"

"Just that there was a sound of water running. Like the time we camped at that campground by the Red Deer River, you know the one by the bridge?"

Will nodded. "Anything else?"

Julie shook her head. "I'm sorry . . . it was so dark. . . ."

"Do your wrists still hurt?"

Julie looked down at her hands. "No," she said, perplexed, "I can move them and they just hurt a little."

"So," said Will, "I expect that he's untied now. Probably means he's locked in somewhere or . . ."

"Or what?"

"Nothing, Punkin," he said, but his voice was tight.

Julie remembered the laboured breathing, looked at his tired face, and decided to say nothing. She struggled out of bed.

Will helped her. "It's only five o'clock but there's no law says you can't have a bit of breakfast. You missed supper last night."

Julie couldn't imagine eating at a time like this, but when she got downstairs and smelled the bacon, she realized that she was ravenous.

The day dragged on. Phone-calls from concerned and curious neighbours were now augmented by calls from reporters. A television crew arrived around noon, in spite of the fact that Paddy Behan said he'd made a point of giving them the wrong directions.

Once in a while some small bit of information came through thanks to Const. Jeffrey Kennedy, who had generously agreed to keep the family posted. In return Mary supplied him with coffee for his thermos and the occasional piece of pie.

Search parties were headquartered in the Hurry town hall, and Paddy Behan had arranged for Hanson's Crop Dusters to fly around taking aerial photographs of any abandoned farms or buildings in the area. The plan was to search every one. A collection had been taken to pay for fuel and other expenses. Mel Hanson was donating his time. And all the while, everyone was watching for a maroon van. There seemed no doubt that the motorcycle and Billy had been loaded into the van McDermid had seen earlier parked by his hayfield.

Will, Charlie, and Jimmy joined the search party after lunch. Mary Behan had come over to help Alice cope with the phone-calls.

Julie tried to find a quiet corner and concentrate on Billy, but there were so many people coming and going, and always there was the barrier of fear that seemed to keep her from him. She was so tired and frightened that it was all she could do to keep from crying.

Jane *was* crying. Sobbing on Mary's shoulder. "It's my fault! I should have stopped him."

"Hey, no . . . don't cry, Jane . . . you couldn't have . . ." Mary's voice was soft, comforting. She rocked her sister.

"That's right," Julie put in, "I tried to stop him, he just got mad at me!"

"You don't understand!" Jane wailed. "He didn't even want Billy . . . he wanted me to go . . . but I wouldn't . . . so he took Billy."

Mary and Alice exchanged looks. Jane was a pretty young girl with long blonde hair. Like the runaway in the barn.

Julie left Mary to cope with her sister. In the kitchen Mary Behan had just hung up the phone. "Well, doesn't that just take the cake!" she said to Alice. "That was Mabel Piggott. Apparently she knows of a psychic in Edmonton she's sure could locate Billy, if we'd just send something of his along for her to 'concentrate' on! Honestly, that woman does beat all!"

Julie said quickly, "Is it okay if I go lie down for a little while, Mum?"

"Alice, you should do the same. You probably didn't get a wink of sleep last night," Mary Behan broke in. "Go along with Julie, I'll call you when Will gets back . . . or if anything . . ."

Alice turned and followed Julie upstairs.

"Why don't you come and lie down with me, Julie? I think we could both use the company."

Julie nodded. "Just a minute, I have to get something."

She slipped in her room and moved the dalmation off the

little stand Billy had carved for it. It was small enough to hold in her hand without Alice noticing. She went and curled up on the bed beside her mother.

Chapter Twenty-two

She could hear it, the sound of water lapping at the bank, rippling, flowing nearby. Again she hovered near the ceiling looking down, but now it was daylight. She could see. Not well, for the only window had been boarded up. But light filtered through the cracks. One small room, a shack, a trapper's cabin, something like that. Rough lumber, darkened by age, festooned with cobwebs all around her. But her attention was focused on the form lying on the old mattress in the corner. Billy.

His breathing was quieter now, but he lay very still. It frightened her. She knew it was useless to try to call him. But perhaps if she thought his name, concentrating hard and staring down at him? She tried and felt a stir of hope as he moved and moaned a little.

Now that she was assured that he was regaining consciousness, she wondered if she had done the right thing. Perhaps he was better off asleep. If he woke up and was trapped here, he would be alone and afraid. And she could do nothing, floating here near the ceiling in a dream. She could only watch.

He moved again and opened his eyes. For a moment he seemed puzzled as he took in his surroundings, then she could see he was remembering and, as she had dreaded, there was fear in his eyes. He got stiffly to his feet, glancing around the room like a trapped animal, his panic palpable.

Julie wanted to cry. She could do nothing. Why had she woken him? He had been better off asleep, oblivious to what had happened. But if I woke him, that was something, wasn't it? I made my thoughts wake him, so he can sense me. Right now I'm terrified along with him, and that's probably making it worse for him. I've got to calm down and help him not to panic.

She concentrated as hard as she could. "I'm here, Billy, sort of anyway . . . you're not alone." She gazed down at him willing him to sense her presence, her thoughts with him. He had stopped staring wildly around him. It was working. He was calmer too. He had moved to the window, quietly checking the boards, to see if there was a loose one.

"Try the door, Billy," she thought, but as he moved toward it, it opened.

The sunlight seemed dazzling, and at first all she could see of the man that entered was the peaked cap he wore pulled down over his eyes. But even without seeing them, she knew instantly that it was the man she had seen in town the week before. So he had been real after all.

It must have taken him a while to adjust to the dim cabin, because he paused at the door as if confused. He obviously hadn't expected Billy to have moved from the mattress.

Julie realized from the grizzled grey hair that showed beneath the cap that the man was much older than his movements showed. And when Billy darted for the door, the man moved much faster than she would have ever given him credit for. Still, Billy almost managed to duck under his arm and escape. He might have wiggled free too, but now there was someone else in the doorway. And Julie recognized him immediately.

"Kid's come out of it faster'n I thought."

Julie watched the men subdue her struggling brother. She could do nothing but watch.

"You got in touch with the others?"

"Yeah," the man in the pony-tail answered. "It's set for tonight. We're stuck here until they come. The cops are looking for the van *or* a motorcycle."

"Damn fool idea, taking a kid with half the family around. Gave us no lead time at all."

"I know, I know," growled the younger man. "You've said it all before. . . . I told you that girl would have been perfect. I didn't even want this one, but I couldn't get rid of him . . . so I figured . . ."

The older man held Billy down while the motorcyclist jabbed a needle in his arm. Soon Billy lay still. Julie felt sick.

"No! no!" she moaned.

Alice was holding her, and she could hear Will's voice.

"Julie, Julie, wake up. You were dreaming again."

Julie opened her eyes. Her hand hurt. She had been squeezing the little wooden stand until the shape of it was deeply imprinted on her palm.

"You were dreaming, Julie . . . about Billy." Will's voice was calm. "Tell me everything you remember about the dream."

Julie looked questioningly at her mother. Once Alice had called her a "changeling child" and Julie knew Alice did not approve of, perhaps even feared, her daughter's strange gifts.

Alice nodded. "Everything," she said.

"Well," Julie began hesitantly, "it was dark the first time. So I couldn't see very well, I could just know he was inside somewhere," her voice caught in her throat, "and hear him breathing. This time," she said, taking a deep breath, "I could see."

Her parents were watching her: Alice staring, her face anxious, Will patiently waiting. It gave her confidence. For the first time in her life, she could share and not be frightened of revealing something of herself she shouldn't.

"He's in a cabin or shack or something. He was sleeping . . . or unconscious, and there were two men. I guess the one Jane saw, with a pony-tail, and a much older man . . . I saw him in town. . . ." She went on telling everything, the sound of running water, what the men said. Everything but the needle. She couldn't say that in front of her mother.

"Was there anything you noticed about the shack, anything else? Try to remember."

Julie paused. "The door," she said, "when it was open. It was so bright but there was writing, or signs . . . or something on it."

"Julie," Will's interest was intense, "do you think you could draw it . . . draw the . . . whatever it was on the door?"

95

Julie nodded. Alice was already fetching a pad of paper and a pencil.

The signs were strange to Julie. Diamonds, odd letters with tangled trailing bits, nothing that made a word of sense. What if they were symbols of something awful . . . Black Magic. . . . Would she be able to draw them?

She found she could. And she could remember most of them, although the door was covered and there were parts she had not been able to see clearly.

Will interrupted her only once at the beginning. "Were they painted on, or carved or what . . . ?"

Julie squeezed her eyes shut, remembering. The marks were deep, but not carved. They looked like some of the things Billy had done with the wood burning kit he got for his birthday last month. "Burned," she said.

Will nodded. "Well, well."

He picked up the paper when Julie had finished and studied it carefully.

Chapter Twenty-three

Julie watched her father as he studied the drawing. "Do you know what these things are, Julie?"

She shook her head, and then, looking in his eyes, knew. "Brands? Cattle brands from branding irons?"

Alice gave a gasp of surprise, "Of course!" She ran her finger over the paper. "There's a double bar none and a lazy K."

Will stood up. "Something to go on, anyway." There was a ring of hope in his voice Julie realized had been missing ever since they had driven home from town that day. Was it only yesterday? "Paddy's got those aerial maps of his, marking off the abandoned buildings. I thought this might be an old granary, but with those brands, we're looking for something in ranch country."

"By a river . . ." added Julie.

Will nodded. "My guess is the Red Deer. The Battle flows too slow even at this time of year. You probably wouldn't hear it."

"How far south did they . . . did Mel Hanson and the others go to take their aerial photographs?" Alice looked worried.

"Not far enough, probably," Will shook his head. "I'll have to see if I can talk them into following the river." He hurried out and was halfway down the stairs before Alice caught up with him.

"Will." Her voice was urgent, pitched deliberately low so Mary Behan and the others in the kitchen wouldn't hear. "What are you going to say? You can't tell anyone about Julie."

They stared at each other.

Will sighed. "You're right. I'll just say it's a hunch on my part." He nodded at the paper in Alice's hand. "And keep that thing under wraps. We may need it."

Alice carefully folded the paper and slipped it into her pocket before she followed Will into the kitchen.

Paddy Behan was there, helping himself to a cup of coffee.

"So Will, did you hear? I guess we have to bless the snoops of this world after all . . . turns out Abbie Lenz never quit collecting licence numbers on any new vehicle she saw around. That maroon van? It was in Hurry a week ago . . ."

"Last Wednesday at 2 P.M. to be exact," put in Mary.

". . . and I guess the fella didn't think to dirty his licence plate that time . . ."

Will grabbed his jacket off the hook by the back door. "I guess we'll have to wait and see if Pearson will tell us who it's registered to, eh?"

Paddy grinned. "Nope. Turns out your daughter here was taking a thermos of coffee out to the cute young constable when they radioed back the information. Turns out it's registered to one Nick Tyler!"

"Old Zach's son!" Alice breathed.

Paddy nodded. "That comes under the heading of bad news . . . bad news."

Will had the door open, his face grim. "Paddy, do you think we can catch Mel and do a bit of flying while there's still a few hours of light left? I can't stand just sitting here."

Back upstairs Alice watched them drive away, her fingers clinging to the folded paper in her pocket. Brands. From branding irons. And if the branding irons had been in the vicinity of that cabin, so were the ranchers that had once used them. She remembered the branding iron on their farm when she was a child. There had been a book, showing the brands and the owners who had registered them. *Brands of Alberta* or something like that. It had been in that box of old books she'd packed up when her father died. She'd donated it to the library in Hurry.

Julie had come out of the bedroom and was just starting down the stairs when Alice grabbed her arm.

"Come on," she said. "We're going to the school . . . to the library. There's something I want to check."

Luckily, Will and Paddy had gone in Behans' car, and although school would be over by the time they got there, Miss Johnson would still be there, at the library.

"I'm just going into town for a little while," she said in answer to Mary Behan's puzzled look. Alice grabbed her purse and ran out of the door.

Ada Johnson's car was there when Alice parked in front of the school. So was another car. Alice Morgan's heart sank. It was Mabel Piggott. Of course, it was Thursday, the library would be open tonight.

Alice sat patiently waiting for Mabel Piggott to leave. At last, in response to the effusive expressions of sympathy, she answered shortly, "Thank you Mabel. I am waiting to speak to Miss Johnson . . . alone!"

"Well, really . . . I was only trying to . . . of course, I know when I'm not wanted. . . ."

Julie watched her snap her purse shut, snatch up the books from Miss Johnson's desk, and stalk out.

Alice waited until the outside door slammed and began, "Ada, you know that old box of books of Dad's we donated? It's years ago, of course, but I noticed some of them . . ."

"Not yet, Mum." Julie was staring expectantly toward the door. It was amazing how quietly a woman of Mabel Piggott's size could walk when she wanted to.

Mrs Piggott had left the door open only a crack. Miss Johnson went and swung it open.

"Did you forget something, Mabel?"

There was no doubt by the way Mabel Piggott jumped back when the door opened, where she had been and what she had been doing. It took her a minute to recover and mumble, "I . . . I came back for my gloves. I must have left them . . ."

"I think you put them in your purse, Mrs. Piggott," Julie said quietly.

There was a short embarrassed snort as the purse was opened and the gloves were retrieved, and they watched Mabel Piggott retreat down the hall.

Miss Johnson stood at the window beside Julie and watched

the car narrowly miss the gatepost as it roared out of the school parking lot before she turned back to Alice.

"Yes, of course, I remember those books. They'll be listed in the Donations File, but if you can remember the title or author, I can just check and see if they're in."

Alice shook her head apologetically. "I'm not sure about the title. . . . It was a book listing all the registered cattle and horse brands for the province of Alberta."

Miss Johnson nodded. "That's back in the storage room with some other old proceedings and registry books from the Land Titles Office that someone donated years ago. I was just looking at them the other day and wondering what to do with them." She hurried out of the room.

Alice had pulled the sheet of paper from her pocket and Julie stood beside her studying it by the time Miss Johnson returned with the book.

"Here it is."

Alice did not look up, but opened the book and began to leaf through it searching for the illustrations of brands that might be similar to the ones on the sketch.

It was Julie who was aware of a sharp intake of breath on Miss Johnson's part and looked up into the librarian's face. The face had paled, but it was not that but an almost electric shock of knowing that hit Julie as if she herself was living the memory passing through Miss Johnson's mind. A boy threatening a little girl with a branding iron as she screamed in fear, the vision ending with the child being bundled up by a woman and taken away.

"This is hopeless," Alice said sadly. "I'll have to go over them one by one." She sighed and handed Miss Johnson the book. "I'll check this out, if I may."

"Certainly." Miss Johnson was all efficiency again. "If it's any help to you, one of those brands is the Circle T. It was used by my uncle, Zachariah Tyler."

Alice's voice betrayed her excitement, though she moved calmly enough, handing Miss Johnson the sketch of brands. "Do you recognize any of the others? Any at all?"

Miss Johnson stared at the sheet, puzzled. "Not really. I may have, of course. There was one fall we went down south at round-up to some land the Tylers had. He ran about a hundred head of cattle down there. His wife was gone, and Mother went down to cook for the crew. I was about six or seven. . . ." She paused and again Julie felt the fear, the panic of a child. "There were several different outfits, each sorting out and branding the cattle that had been running together."

Alice had been listening intently, staring at Miss Johnson, as if afraid to speak or break into the train of thought.

"You know," said Ada Johnson, indicating the sheet, "this sort of reminds me of the cook shack door. I guess it was sort of a tradition to burn on all the different brands from the out-fits that were there. Isn't that strange, I should remember that after all these years? That door. Mind you that place was associated with some unpleasant memories. . . ." She paused. "It was the last time we had anything to do with the Tylers. The last time I saw my cousin Nicodemus." She turned away and walked to the window, and Julie barely heard her now. She was speaking as if to herself. "Thank God," she said.

Alice Morgan was speaking now, words pouring out, tumbling over each other in her haste to be gone. ". . . Close the library . . . come with us . . . where? How far?"

Before Julie knew it, they were in the car, heading for the search headquarters, Miss Johnson's protestations drowned by Alice's insistence.

"I was only seven, I couldn't find the place again. . . ."

And Alice saying tensely, "We've got to find it, there's not that much time. Who would know where Tyler's other land was?"

Both women spoke at once: "Gil Gordon!" Alice made a U-turn right in the middle of Hurry's main street and sped off to the amazement of Const. Kennedy, who had just come out of the detachment office.

Chapter Twenty-four

Billy's first thought as he groped his way back to consciousness was water. He could hear it and he was thirsty. He'd never been so thirsty.

Gradually his eyes adjusted to the dim light inside the shack. There was a canteen sitting on the floor beside him. He didn't think that had been there before. Somebody had been here and eaten something. There were crumbs and a sandwich crust being nibbled by a mouse beside his foot. He was glad there were no rats in Alberta.

He listened carefully, but he couldn't hear any voices outside. Still, he knew the two men would still be here. Hadn't they said they couldn't go anywhere? That the vehicles were being watched for?

At last he sat up. It took all his effort not to moan. His head felt awful, his legs and arms cramped from lying immobile for so long. Slowly he flexed his fingers, moving his limbs one by one, getting the circulation going again. Even at that, when he finally stood, it was with a grimace of pain, and the dizziness almost made him lie down again. He waited to be sure that he had not been heard, listening for footsteps outside the door.

He could tell by the shaft of sunlight through the cracks that it was still day. But what day? When had he had the last needle? They'd mentioned midnight. People coming at midnight Thursday for him. Well, he was still here but there probably wasn't that much time. The sun set around ten o'clock. At least it did at home. No telling how far south they'd come. He remembered that much after the motorcycle ride had turned from fun to fear to pain when he'd tried to run and hide in the ditch.

But the man in the van had come, and they'd held him down and jabbed his arm. Just before that though, the ponytailed one—Ron he'd said his name was, when he was being so friendly and nice back in Hurry—had said, "We're taking him to the place down south you talked about, right?" And Billy guessed the other one had agreed or nodded or something, but he was too busy struggling trying to get away to have noticed.

He tried to swallow, and remembered how parched and sore his throat was. He moved over to the wall behind the door and put his eye to the largest of the cracks. He couldn't see much, but there was Ron beside the motorcycle, polishing the chrome. Now he could hear voices, the older man's voice.

"You better keep that thing and yourself outta sight."

"What the hell for? We're miles from the road. You could hardly see the trail we came in on."

"I saw some canoers going by earlier, probably heading down to Morrin or Drumheller. Bad enough if they were to see the shack and decide it was a good place to camp or have lunch. Bloody river's turning into some kind of recreational zone. Used to be so peaceful here . . . except at round-up . . . then there was some doin's." He had moved forward and Billy could see him now. "I'll just check on the kid. By the way, when you phoned did you tell him you didn't get a girl?"

"Yeah, and it don't matter that much . . . just so's it's young. Young blood . . . that's what he said."

"Oh yeah?" The man's voice became slippery. "How old did you say you were, Ronny?"

"Shut up! you old . . ."

Billy supposed there had been some threatening movement with the last words, but he was back on the mattress trying to remember exactly what position his arms and legs had been in when he woke up. He heard the sound of key in padlock and the latch thrown back.

"Just kidding, Ronny," the same wheedling voice, ". . . but the heat's going to be on for a while, and it'd be a shame to have to go back to calves . . ." Something hit the door. "Hey," the voice was alarmed now, "I *said* I was kidding!"

"Well, dammit, don't!"

The door creaked open. "Hey kid!"

Billy didn't move. He tried to keep his breathing soft and shallow, his eyes from flickering. If a person's unconscious, he wondered, is he stiff or limp? He felt a boot nudge his shoulder none too gently and opted for limp.

"He's still out. He should be coming around soon. D'ya think we should give him something to eat?"

"What the hell for? He'll be dead in six hours or so." The door closed and Billy lay there. He began to shake and breathe in deep gasping breaths. Six hours. It must be six o'clock already.

Alice wished Will was along, but she couldn't wait any longer. She'd left him a note and a scrawled map that Gil Gordon had drawn. "Now you know, Alice, roads change over the years, and this was just a range trail. Maybe the county road's changed too and it'll be even worse, but here's how I remember it . . . the fall I rode with old Zach's crew. Probably wouldn't remember the way in at all, but I used to ride over to Rowley once in a while in the evening and had to find my way back across country. So I memorized the landmarks. Trees and fences change but the hills and rocks'll still be there . . . maybe."

There could be no maybe's as far as Alice was concerned.

Julie sat in the back seat with Miss Johnson. They had just crossed the Nevis bridge. "I hate to be the one to bring this up, but what do we do when we get there? If it's Nicodemus there's no telling what he'll do. . . ." Her voice hardened. "He had a mean streak even as a child."

"I'm hoping, by the time we get there, Paddy and Will will have got my message and Mel will fly them down. It should be easy to follow us from the air, with the map. And Mary was to give us a head start and then go to Const. Kennedy with her copy of the map. I just didn't want to do it before we left, in case . . ."

Mr. Gordon chuckled, ". . . In case he wouldn't let you go off on this wild goose chase! I want you to know that I'm only along because Will would never forgive me if I let you and Ada and young Juliet there go traipsing off on your own." His expression became grim. "And because if it really is Nick Tyler, then you could be on to something . . . and because we've got to find young William!"

Julie leaned back in the seat. The little wooden stand was in her jeans pocket cutting into her. She slipped it out, held it against her cheek, and closed her eyes.

Billy still lay on the mattress, but suddenly his panic seemed to leave him. He had to get out of there. Six o'clock, three or four hours before sunset. But then it wouldn't be dark for another hour or two, not dark enough to hide anyway, even if he could get out of here. By the time it was really dark it would be midnight and too late. The thought almost made him panic again, but he knew he couldn't. If only he wasn't alone . . . and yet somehow he didn't feel alone.

What was it Julie always said? You can't be lonely because you carry everything you ever knew with you all the time. So what did he know? That he had to get out of this shack and hide somewhere until dark. Sure. But he also knew that the window was boarded up with spikes that he couldn't have pulled out without a pinch bar, and that the door was padlocked, and that he was outnumbered.

He got up and began to check the corners of the shack. Some old gunny sacks and a torn blanket in one corner gave him an idea. If he *could* get out it would be smart to not let them know when they first looked in. He took off his shirt and began to stuff it with bits of blanket. Then he arranged it on the mattress with a gunny sack cover and another sack rolled up underneath. It sort of looked like somebody lying there. Somebody without a head, of course, that would be a problem—unless he moved the mattress or made it look like the person had moved so that their head was off the edge. It wouldn't fool anybody for very long anyway.

Now if this was like movies or T.V., he'd just hide behind the door when they came in and duck out while they walked over to the dummy like they didn't notice anybody dodging by them. Trouble was, he knew that wouldn't work, and besides they seldom came in together. He didn't think there'd be any more needles. Not this close to . . . to midnight. He could feel

105

the panic start again. Calm down Billy. Think about what you know. What do I know? That I'm just a kid against two grown men twice my size. So make it work for you. . . . Right, I can go where they can't. He stopped and looked up, searching the ceiling for a hole or some way out. There was the old stove pipe. A wonder it hadn't fallen down when the stove was taken out. Now if he could just get up there and get it out, he might be able to squeeze through. And the roof wouldn't be a bad place to hide if he lay flat. Except, of course, they'd notice the hole, and then there was the little detail of getting up there.

There was a wooden box in one corner, sort of a crate, and Billy began to drag it away to stand on. If only they wouldn't check on him again for a while.

Chapter Twenty-five

"**I** can't believe Alice would take off on a wild goose chase like this by herself," Paddy Behan grumbled to Will as they herded Mel Hanson back to the plane.

"She wasn't by herself," Will said.

"Sure, great little team of vigilantes she's rounded up: a librarian, a kid, and an old coot!"

"Gil Gordon may be gettin' on but he's nobody's fool. If he remembers something about old Zach Tyler's place down south, it could be just what we need to know."

"Sure, and Ada Johnson remembers a door with brands on it! What's that got to do with anything?"

Will wished he hadn't let Paddy see Alice's note, but it was too late now. "Just a hunch," he said shortly.

"We've got maybe two more hours of daylight before the shadows get too long to see right," Mel announced as he climbed in.

Will and Paddy were already buckled in.

"Alice left about six. It'll take about two hours, an hour and a half tops to get there."

"Yeah. And if this map is right then we didn't follow the river far enough. Okay if we go down from Nevis and see if we see anything? We can cut across to No. 21 and track Alice down then."

Mel Hanson nodded. "If the cabin's still there and it's by the river we should be able to see it." The Cessna bumped over Mel's dirt runway and took off.

"Your mother has no business taking off like that," Jeffrey

107

Kennedy told Mary. "You mean to say she's been gone for an hour, and you are just getting around to telling me?"

Mary wished she were home. She'd been looking forward to having an excuse to see him and now he was . . . well, he was obviously upset with her . . . he wasn't exactly yelling but . . . what gave him the right, anyway? "Mum told me to wait for Daddy but . . . well, I got worried . . . so I came here." She stared at him. "Aren't you harrassing a witness or something?"

He grinned. "Probably. But if you want to see harrassing, wait until you see what Sgt. Pearson does to me. Especially since I'm taking you with me and following your mother."

"Isn't that against regulations?" Mary smiled. Things had definitely taken a change for the better. Besides, she couldn't bear the thought of sitting doing nothing.

"Probably," he said opening the patrol car door for her, "but I can't read Mr. Gordon's handwriting, so I need a navigator."

"It's true, I've had a few years experience trying to figure out the comments on my essays!" She wanted to laugh, to savour the feeling of being with him, but she felt guilty even thinking about it when Billy wasn't safe. It wasn't fair.

"The sergeant will be meeting us at the Nevis bridge. He's coming from Red Deer, so we'd better move it. In the meantime, just to make conversation and pass the time, I understand that your graduation dance is less than a month away and . . . well, I don't know what the custom is hereabouts but . . . I've booked off that night in case you needed an escort or anything. . . ."

"It's not surprising I guess, Alice, but things have changed a fair bit in fifty years." Gil Gordon mopped his forehead and squinted at the sun. "What time's it getting on for, Ada?"

Alice was carefully backing out of another hayfield roadway they'd been creeping along in an effort to find the river.

"Nearly 7:30. Let's go back and try that other one a couple of miles back." Alice sighed. "I guess we can't do worse. Julie still sleeping?"

Mr. Gordon turned his head and stared at Julie. "Funny, how

the kid can sleep through all of this bumping along the back roads," he said thoughtfully. "You know Alice, I think if the road Ada suggested doesn't work, you'd better wake her up."

Alice gave him a startled look, realized he was staring at her speculatively, and turned back to her driving. What does he know about Julie? she wondered.

Even as Billy had pulled the wooden crate away he'd known that it was hopeless. He'd never be able to reach the stove-pipe hole. Twice the voices had got so loud he'd thought the men were coming into the shack, and he'd shoved the box back and crawled under the sacks just in case. The box was heavy and awkward to move and he had to be quiet, and as he lay back on the dirty mattress he just wanted to quit. But somehow he couldn't. Try again! Don't give up! he kept thinking over and over. This time he managed to tug the box halfway to the middle of the floor. Slow going. Pull on one end, then go to the other and push. Half an inch at a time, it seemed to take forever. He was so busy concentrating on the box and being quiet that he didn't notice the corner it came from. A hole, where the wood had rotted away and something had dug under. Not a very big hole but then he was a skinny kid and if he dug a little more . . . He worked as fast as he could. If he could just squeeze his shoulders through. And it would help if he could pull the box back a little, so they wouldn't notice anything different at first. . . . For the first time he let himself believe that he had a chance of getting out of here. He began to squeeze through the hole. Just his luck, must have been dug by a skunk. Oh well, at least the varmint wasn't home right now.

Alice backed the car down the narrow ruts of yet another dead end road. She wanted to put her head down on the steering wheel and weep, but that never did anybody any good. Keep going, Alice.

"Do you hear anything, Gilbert?" Ada Johnson had been peering intently out the back window, trying to see the sky. "I thought I heard a plane . . . just wishful thinking perhaps," she sighed.

Mr. Gordon had reached over into the back and shook Julie's arm. "All right, young Juliet! Wake up!"

Julie opened her eyes. Her mouth felt unbearably dry, her sides scraped as if she'd been crawling through spaces too small and rough for her skin.

Const. Kennedy had been right about the sergeant's reaction. Worse still because there was another constable from the Red Deer detachment with him when the police cars rendezvoused at the bridge.

"What do you mean, bringing that girl along?" he hissed when he stuck his head in the window of the Hurry patrol car. Mary knew he'd have said a lot more if she hadn't been sitting there. "Will Morgan's not going to appreciate . . ." he began and then to Mary, ". . . your father is going . . ."

"My father is going to know that I am perfectly safe with you and Const. Kennedy, Sgt. Pearson." Mary smiled sweetly at him. "But I don't think he'd like it if you didn't take me with you," she looked around innocently. "I don't think I could find my way home from here!"

Dan Pearson gave her a look of resignation, glared at his constable, and said, "I'll deal with you later." He turned abruptly. "Now let's get moving and see how far that map takes us."

Alice didn't dare look at Julie as she climbed into the middle of the front seat at Mr. Gordon's request.

Gil Gordon was staring out the window. "You know Miss Juliet-of-the-Spirits, your old Celtic great-grandmother was famous in our district for water-witchin' . . . dowsing, some people call it. She once took a willow branch and walked through our yard . . . I was a kid and I watched her. When she got to the spot where the water was, it sort of pulled in her hands. Sure enough, we dug and got water right there." He rubbed his chin thoughtfully. "She left the stick behind and I tried to use it, but nothing ever happened. It wasn't the stick . . . it was the person holding it." He looked over at Julie. "I figure we've got to be pretty close and there aren't many fences in this country. . . ." He took Julie's hand and put it on the steering wheel between Alice's. "Shut your eyes, concentrate on your brother, . . . *and steer!*"

"Gilbert Gordon! Have you taken leave of your senses!" Miss Johnson's voice had a shocked timbre to it.

"Get off your high horse for a minute, Ada my dear, you know as well as I do that young Juliet here has never been exactly an average child. Now we'll find out just how exceptional she is! Besides," he added in a more subdued tone, "we've about reached the end of what *we* can do."

Alice took a deep breath. She wasn't sure what she intended to say, but she knew she'd better say something to defuse the situation and get Julie off the hook. "Now, Gil," she began and then felt the steering wheel jerk in her hands. Julie was pulling it sharply to the right towards a stand of scrub. It was rough going and she had to concentrate on steadying the car without going too much against the way Julie seemed to be directing.

"Easy, Julie," she said softly. "Just let me steer around these trees." They moved into the clearing on the other side.

"That's it!" Mr. Gordon was pointing ahead to a faintly discernible track on the grass. "There's been a vehicle through here in the last day or two. So now all we have to do is follow the track. Though what," he added under his breath, "we're going to do when we get there is anybody's guess."

Chapter Twenty-six

Billy lay spreadeagled on the roof. His first impulse when he got out of the shack had been to run for it. But the bush wasn't thick enough to hide in, and the first place they'd look was by the river. Besides, how far could he run? He didn't know where the roads were or where he was. "What do you know?" he thought and remembered reading somewhere that sometimes the best place to hide something was in the most obvious place. If he lay still, they wouldn't see him, they wouldn't be able to climb up here, the roof would cave in. He'd thought for a minute it was going to go just with his weight, which was why he was spreading himself around as much as he could. So far they hadn't come inside so they weren't looking for him. He could hear a plane, flying low, coming nearer . . . too bad he'd left his shirt inside, he could signal. No. That wouldn't work, he'd better not even try waving. The plane would make the men look up, and they'd see any movement on the roof. The plane was just about overhead now, but he couldn't even lift his head enough to see it. Boy, it *was* low. Maybe there was a chance of them noticing him and telling somebody. He could move an arm if he kept it flat against the roof.

"How much farther south do you want to go, Will?" Mel Hanson banked the plane slightly following the curve of the river. "We'll be at the Morrin bridge in another few minutes."

Will's attention did not shift from the river bank below. "I guess that'll have to do. No. 27 crosses there, doesn't it?" He sighed, "We'll backtrack from there and locate Alice."

"You know, I've seen more of this country today than I have

in a whole lifetime of living here." Paddy Behan's voice rose. "Flying this low, you can even see the coyotes."

Will's voice was flat. "Not the coyotes we're looking for!"

"I used to fly pipelines. Low altitude flying's my favourite," said Mel. "That's how come I ended up dusting, I guess."

"Just a minute!" Paddy was pointing to the west bank of the river below him. "There's something! . . . some guys . . . a shack . . ."

". . . And a maroon van!" Mel's voice echoed Paddy's excitement.

"Damn . . ." Paddy exulted. "We've found 'em!"

Will said nothing. His attention was focused on the roof of the shack and the body spreadeagled there.

"Wait a minute . . . look at that! Isn't that Billy? What have they done to him?" There was horror in Paddy's voice. ". . . Crucified him or something, the sons of . . ."

Will cut him off. His voice hard and calm and no nonsense, "He's all right . . . ," and more softly, ". . . he's got to be all right!"

Mel was busy banking the plane sharply, bringing it around to make another pass over the shack.

On the first fly-by, the two men below had stood transfixed, staring up, but this time they were moving, one running for the van, the other towards the door of the little cabin.

"There, you see!" Will's voice, still even, held an immense relief, ". . . he's moving his arm! He's all right!"

There was relief and triumph in Paddy's voice as well. "By damn you're right! But what's he doing up there, if they didn't put him there?"

Below them, as the plane banked to begin another turn, the man came running out of the cabin, ran around it as if looking for something, then glancing upward, ran toward the van that had already backed around and started to drive away.

"That's it! They're on the run!" Mel turned to Will, "I guess Billy's all right if we follow them?"

Paddy Behan was laughing, shaking his head. "By damn, I'll bet that's what he's doing . . . he's hiding up there. Smart kid!"

"Yeah," said Will smiling.

The van was bumping up the steep bank and out into an open stretch just as another vehicle came into view heading towards it.

"Great Caesar's ghost!" shouted Paddy. "It's Alice!"

Will tensed. "Can you set this thing down anywhere here Mel? If they . . . ?"

". . . Not a chance, too rough . . ." Mel Hanson shook his head. "But if they stop and try anything . . . taking hostages or whatever, I'll crash land damn soon." He banked again, turning and swooping low over the van once more. "Let's see if I can keep 'em running."

Alice braked the car sharply. They'd seen and recognized Mel Hanson's plane with relief. But now the van speeding toward her made her fears live again. Were they taking Billy away? She could see the faces of the men in the plane clearly as they buzzed the van. Before she could react, the van veered sharply around her and sped by on up the bank.

It was pure impulse but she gunned the motor and began to turn to follow.

"No," said Julie, grabbing the steering wheel again. "Billy's not in there."

Alice braked and pulled the car around without a word, steering it slowly and carefully in the direction from which the van had come.

Billy lay on the roof, the setting sun warming his bare back, listening to the sound of the plane's motor diminish. After he heard Ron yelling down below, "The kid's gone," and the other man telling him to forget it and get the hell out of there, he'd dared to lift his head just enough to see the van driving away. He didn't think they'd come back but wasn't sure if it would be safe to climb down just yet.

Then he heard something else. A car coming back. Not the van, a familiar motor, and there was the familiar green Chev bumping down the bank. He began scrambling down the roof, risking falling through, scraping half the skin off his chest. But it was worth it to see their faces as he strolled around the side of the shack. His heart was beating so hard he thought it would break right out of his chest, but he wasn't letting on as the car doors flew open and his mother and sister raced towards him.

Alice's hug nearly muffled it, but he managed to break loose long enough to turn to Julie.

"What took you?" he said.

Chapter Twenty-seven

It was nearly midnight by the time they were all back at the Morgan farm. Statements had been taken, and with Mary's help the family were just beginning to sort out the day's events.

"I don't think it's fair that you were the one who got to be there at the end," Joe complained to Mary. "You don't even like watching chase scenes on T.V."

"It must have been neat," Jane put in, ". . . when Hanson landed the plane on the road on one side of the van, and you guys in the cop cars were coming from the other side . . ."

"Yeah," Jimmy agreed, "I'd like to have seen that!"

"Well, actually, I didn't see that part. Jeffrey made me promise to get down on the floor, in case there was shooting. I think he was really sorry he'd taken me along. He was mumbling about how maybe regulations made sense after all and if anything happened to me . . ."

"She's blushing!" shrieked Jane. "Quick! Get the hose, get the cold water . . . !"

"Isn't it past your bedtime?" said Mary trying not to laugh.

Julie lay in bed later staring at the dark ceiling. She looked forward to seeing Billy tomorrow. It was too bad he'd had to stay overnight at the hospital for observation, but Alice had insisted on spending the night in his room. "I'm not letting that boy out of my sight!" she'd said.

Julie knew she needn't worry about Billy. And she wasn't worried about dreaming tonight either. She'd replaced the little wooden stand under the dalmation on the shelf with the other dogs.

Only one thing bothered her. The circle was widening. How many people could know a secret before it was no longer a secret? People who knew your secrets owned a piece of you. Did that diminish you? She had been relieved when her parents knew. It made it easier somehow, not to be hiding things from them, to know that they understood some of her confusion. Now the circle included Mr. Gordon and Miss Johnson and maybe even Billy. They were people who cared: giving the comfort of their knowing, taking the strength of her solitude.

She remembered hearing Mr. Gordon offer to drive Miss Johnson home and had watched from the window as he opened the car door for her and helped her in. What was it Mr. Behan had said? "High time those two got back together, must be twenty-five years since they broke their engagement."

Everybody has secrets, she thought. She could feel herself drifting off to sleep, light and soft as a shadow. Floating. And pieces of her fell away like flakes of snow.

About the Author

Cora Taylor was born at Fort Qu'Appelle, Saskatchewan, and spent her childhood on her grandmother's farm near Carlton. In 1968 she returned to school to study English and took story-writing, play-writing, and film-writing courses under such masters as W. O. Mitchell and Rudy Wiebe. She has published several magazine articles, is the author of two musical plays, and has had her work broadcast on CBC Radio. She is actively involved with the Edmonton Branch of the Canadian Authors' Association, and was editor of the *Alberta Poetry Yearbook* from 1980 to 1987.

Cora is a widow and has four children, four stepchildren, and fifteen grandchildren. She currently raises donkeys, chickens, dogs, and a goose on an acreage just outside Edmonton.

Julie's Secret is her third book written for children. Her first, *Julie*, won the Canada Council Children's Literature Prize, the 1985 Canadian Library Association's Book of the Year for Children Award, and the Alberta Writers' Guild R. Ross Annett Award for Children's Literature. Her second, *The Doll*, won the Canadian Children's Book Centre Choice Award and the Ruth Schwartz Children's Book Award.